Payback

SALLY A. ALLEN

ISBN Softcover   978-1-950580-19-4

Printed in the United States of America.

To order additional copies of this book, contact:
Bookwhip
1-855-339-3589
https://www.bookwhip.com

CHAPTER

1

When the steel gates clanked behind him, Rock Rayburn walked slowly out into the midday sun, the brightest he had seen for the ten long years he was in prison. The injustice of it all grew larger in his mind each day like a cancer.

His clothes hung on his small, muscular frame, the result of the many hours he'd spent in the gym working out. He swiped at his wrinkled pants trying to straighten the grooves made by years of being stuffed in a plastic bag. His visor cap was dirty and misshapen.

As Rock walked to the road, dismay washed over him. What would he do and where would he go? It was doubtful he could get a job anywhere and no one was waiting for him. He cursed out loud at the four men that were responsible for his dilemma and the pay backs were the only thing on his mind. He vowed to kill each of them one by one, making them suffer before he imposed the final fatal act. "God knows," he thought viciously as he shuddered at the idea. He was overcome with bitterness at the thought of the 'Dear John' letter he had gotten from Ellen the second year he was in prison. The crumpled note was stuffed in the pocket of his jeans to remind him of what happened, even though he could never forget. He should punish her too, but his fondness for her still lingered.

Rock found himself facing the asphalt road that passed by the prison. Which way should he go? It really didn't make much difference but it was useless to go back to the place he was born and raised because everyone knew him there. All the people in the small town were nervous about a convicted felon being released from prison and coming back to live amongst them. Rock would be damned if he would go back there so he stuck out his thumb to hitch a ride going the opposite direction. After several cars sped up to pass him, he realized he'd have to get away from the front of the prison.

He shuffled slowly along the road in the direction of Summerville, a sizeable town a fellow could get lost in. After about five miles, the scorching sun was getting to him and he was tired and hungry. His last meal had been the day before and was only shit on a shingle, a meal he detested.

Suddenly an eighteen wheeler came down the road, doin' about sixty miles an hour. When the driver saw Rock, he laid on the horn so he stuck his thumb out hopefully. To his amazement, the big rig pulled over and stopped. With his heart pounding, Rock ran toward the truck. The driver leaned over and opened the passenger door, "Hop in," he yelled. "I recon you are sick and tired of hoofin' it."

Rock hoisted himself up into the cab of the truck and gratefully said, "Thanks man!"

The trucker merely nodded and replied, "I've walked a mile in your shoes buddy. My name's Big Jim; what's yours?"

Rock hesitated "Stoner," he replied lying.

"Sure it is," Jim said smiling. "Try again."

"It's really Rock and that's the truth."

"Okay, Rock, where yah goin'?"

"Anywhere, no-where, I don't really much care."

"It's that way is it? No relatives or friends to help you?"

Rock shook his head, "Nope, neither one."

"Look," Jim said, "I'm an ex-con too, been out of prison seven years. I got caught with a stolen gun which had been used in a murder. Hell, I bought it off the street. I ain't a killer."

"I know exactly what you mean. I took the rap for some other guy's crime too and spent ten years in a hell-hole because of it."

"I hear yah. I did fourteen years myself. I'll tell you one thing for sure though, put it behind you and keep your nose clean. After a while it will seem like the whole thing happened to someone else."

"Sure it will," Rock jeered sarcastically.

"Believe what you want, but take my advice. Remember, I've been there, done that. The two men were quiet until they approached the outskirts of Summerville. "Where should I drop yah?" Jim asked.

"The next corner is as good as any. I see there's a watering hole there. I want to get falling down drunk!"

Big Jim slammed on the brakes. "No you don't. You'll get your ass in deep shit again if you do. I'll tell you what; I'm goin' up to a truck stop a couple miles up the road. Come with me and get a hot shower, a meal in your belly and crash for a while. I have to leave early because my load is due in Chicago by tomorrow night. I'll be gone before you get up, but I wish you luck." He pulled a hundred dollar bill out of his pocket. "Here take it, for a start anyway. Then you're on your own."

Rock went in with him to get a room and joined him for a roast beef dinner. When they were finished the two men shook hands and went their separate ways. Rock would always be grateful to the man. Loneliness washed over him as he realized he was really on his own now.

CHAPTER

2

At first it was difficult to get to sleep in the bedroom at the truck-stop. The trucker's chatter was loud because of the thin, plywood walls. Doors slammed as they came and went from the bunk house. The sound of water running in the showers and toilets flushing was constant.

Rock tossed and turned, finally falling into a fit-full sleep. His reoccurring nightmare came again. He broke into a cold sweat as the image of the cops pulling him over on a speeding violation and the fiasco that followed flooded his mind. Rock was ordered out of the car after he couldn't produce a registration of the vehicle. To make things worse, after the State Patrol called in, they discovered the car was stolen. He was thrown against the car and frisked by one officer while another forced open the trunk and found four bags of money and then was roughly stuffed into the squad car and taken to jail. The nightmare caused Rock to sit up in bed trembling and dripping with sweat. Each time the dream became more real. The irony was that he should take the fall for the other three guys to boot. For the thousandth time he vowed to pay each of them back for lying, resulting in Rock's ten long years in prison. He would seek them out and take care of them one by one. He didn't know just how yet, but he knew he must do everything different in each case so the acts wouldn't be connected.

As usual the nightmare lingered and he was sure his sleep was over for the night so he put on his wrinkled clothing and went out for a walk to explore the place. Everything was quiet now because most drivers had left very early to be able to reach destinations to drop their loads on time.

One cubby was occupied with a burly man snoring loudly. Rock peered into the small room and he saw a uniform hanging on a rack near the door. His heart raced when he saw the opportunity to steal some new clothes. Looking the trucker over, he decided the body under the blanket was about his size. Quietly he entered the room, tip-toeing to the wall the clothes were hanging on and jerked them off the the pegs. The figure in the bed rolled over and stopped snoring. Rock froze. However the man began snoring again so he took the opportunity to run from the room with the stolen clothes under his arm.

Back in his own room, he took off his old clothes and struggled into the others. They fit except the pants were too short and only came to just above his ankles and the belt was tight even though it was in the last notch. The plain flannel shirt was a good fit. What the Hell, he thought, this change was good enough. After collecting his money from the pocket of his old jeans he left the room. Rock quickened his step when he heard the other trucker awake and curse loudly, obviously seeing that his clothes were gone. He stopped just long enough to get a cup of coffee from the machine on the table at the end of the hall. He walked through the door and stood by the side of the building wondering what he should do now. Out of the corner of his eye he saw a trucker walk out of the bunk house dressed in his old clothes. The man stomped over to the only truck left in the lot. The loud engine roared as he drove away.

Rock sighed with relief as he walked in front of the truck-stop's restaurant that was brightly lit. It was only six o'clock in the morning. When he reached the road he decided to hitch again but there wasn't much traffic that early, so he walked until he spotted an all-night diner, and decided to get some breakfast. God only knew when he'd eat again.

Because it was so early there were only a few men seated at the counter. They were obviously men on their way to work as every one of them had a lunch box sitting beside them. Rock sat down next to them and ate a stack of pancakes with bacon and eggs. Satisfied with the meal, he paid the bill and headed toward the door. Looking up, he saw some t-shirts and sweatshirts displayed on the wall with twenty-nine, ninety-eight printed on a sign below them. "What the Hell", he thought. The morning was chilly and he could use a warm sweatshirt, so he purchased a blue one. Mel's Diner was printed across the front. When he got outside he pulled it over his head as he walked to the road.

There was more traffic now so he stuck out his thumb, and to his surprise an old pick-up pulled over. He opened the door and saw a middle aged man sitting in the driver's seat.

"Howdy," the man said in a friendly voice. "Need a ride, huh?"

"Yup," Rock answered. "My car ran out of gas awhile back and I need a ride to a gas station."

"Ain't that a bitch? It happened to me once. I made sure it never happened again."

"Where you headed," Rock asked.

"I'm just driving down the road a piece, then turning around and driving back to the factory where I work. It's only a mile down the road and every morning I come to the seven-eleven and grab a cup of coffee and a donut before I go to work."

"What kind of a factory is it?" Rock asked.

"One that makes car parts. It doesn't pay much, but a job is a job. Almost everyone in the area works there. This is a poor county and work is hard to get."

Rock's interest perked up. "I could use a job. My job back home was fazed out because of lack of business. Do they happen to need any help?"

The driver mused and then replied, "They just might. An old man that had worked there twenty-five years just retired because his health was failing. You could apply for his job but it's only on the assembly line and pays minimum wage. However, they are busy and any ambitious guy can get as much overtime as he wants."

Anything to make a little cash sounded good to Rock. The hundred dollars he had is going fast and won't last much longer. "Mind if I go in with you and put in an application?"

"Why not," the man answered. "The office is right in front of the factory." He looked at Rock surprised and asked, "What about your car man?"

"Oh, I'll get some gas and pick it up later. No one would want the old clunker so I can leave it there for a while."

The man seemed satisfied with Rock's answer so he grinned and said, "Got-cha!" After driving for another mile he turned into a driveway that led to a sprawling concrete building, the parking lot filled with cars. The driver stopped the pick-up in front of the factory. He pointed, "Just go in, the office is right there. Good luck!"

When Rock jumped out of the truck he waved at the man, "Thanks," he said.

"Anytime," the man answered and drove to the parking lot. Rock watched him leave and realized he didn't even know the man's name.

CHAPTER

3

The office was busy with telephones ringing. It had two desks with a woman sitting at each one. The women were busy filing or typing on the computer. Rock walked up to the first desk, "Hello," he said. "Could I have an application, please?"

"Sure," the girl replied, opening the desk drawer and pulling out a sheet of paper which she handed to Rock. "Fill it in and I'll see that the personnel department gets it." The woman was about Rock's age and pretty with strawberry blonde hair. Rock's groin tickled; he hadn't been with a woman for so long that any woman would look good to him. He turned away and sat down grabbing a magazine from the table to put the application on, filling out most of the questions but he lied about an address and previous employment. He made up a fictitious name of a steel plant up North in Pittsburgh. He doubted if the company would check out his employment from one that far away. He wrote that he worked there ten years then handed the paper back to the girl.

She scanned it over and asked, "What are you doing here? You're a long way from Pittsburg."

Rock thought quickly. "I have an elderly aunt who lives here and is not in good health. She lives on social security and can't afford her medical payments. I plan on staying to help her out but I need a job to make some money."

"How nice of you," the woman said obviously impressed. "I see you have an impressive work record too. Let me call in the personnel manager." She pressed a button and soon an older, nice looking man with glasses came in from an adjoining office.

"What is it Cathy?" he asked. She gestured toward Rock.

"Ken, I think you should look at this application. It's better than any we've gotten so far," and handed it to the man.

He looked it over quickly and invited Rock into his office. When Rock was settled, the man bluntly stated, "You must be used to earning a good wage, but we only start you out at minimum wage here. A new employee is subject to a thirty-day evaluation and if they pass, they will be permanently employed. The hourly wage is low but we offer a lot of overtime." He looked Rock in the eye, "What do you think?" Rock repeated the same story he'd used on the woman in the office. "That's commendable. Could you start immediately?"

Rock couldn't believe his good luck. "Sure," he replied, then added, "Thank you, sir."

"Come back here at eight o'clock in the morning and a foreman will show you the ropes. I'm sure you will find it an easy job to learn. However it is rather boring. You will inspect parts to be sure they aren't defective. Exciting isn't it?" he grinned.

"I thank you for the opportunity, sir."

"See you tomorrow then," Ken said dismissing him.

Rock left with a smile on his face. When he passed through the office, he waved at Cathy. "See you tomorrow," he said happily.

He knew he had to find a place to stay and walked for a while until he found a small Mom and Pop motel. It was freshly painted a white color with green trim and had a vacancy sign in the window. "Perfect," Rock said and walked in the front door.

An older, gray haired lady stood behind the counter. When she saw him, she broke into a smile and asked, "Can I help you?"

"I'm in need of a room for a couple nights until I find a permanent place to stay."

"You're not from here are you?"

"No, but I intend to stay awhile. This morning I got hired at Park Products."

"That's a great place to work, you'll like it there. You also need a place to stay you said?"

"I do, and not knowing the town, I don't know where to look."

"Maybe I can help you with that. I have a friend that runs a boarding house not far from here. She offers small apartments with living room, bedroom, kitchen and bath. They aren't large but for a single man like you it's great." The expression on her face asked if he was alone.

"Oh, yeah I'm a bachelor. I never seem to find the right woman."

She winked at him. "If you're looking for a squeeze there's plenty of pretty women around here."

Rock tried to look unenthusiastic. "I like to find 'em myself, but if I don't, I'll let you direct me to one."

"That's a deal! She reached under the counter and produced a key. "Here's the key to room 101. It's not fancy but we keep it nice and clean."

The next day Rock got up early anxious to get to his new job. It would be wonderful to make some money so he could buy some new clothes and a car in time.

CHAPTER

4

The foreman took Rock on a tour of the factory. The work area bustled with activity as men stood at a long work table sorting through auto parts. After careful inspection the good ones continued along the conveyer belt and the rejects were pulled off the line and put into a bin.

The job looked like a piece of cake to Rock but he hoped it wouldn't be too boring. However, the day passed quickly and it was four o'clock before he knew it. He had two bins filled by the end of the day and the supervisor seemed pleased with him.

Erma, the woman at the motel, gave Rock the address of her friend, Beatrice Simmons' apartment. That would be an easy walk from work. A woman about sixty-eight years old answered the door. "Mr. Morrison, I assume," she greeted him.

"One and the same, Ma'am," Rock returned.

"Come in, come in. I'll show you the apartment; I think it'll fit your needs." He followed her up a short flight of stairs and stopped at a freshly painted door. She took out a key from her apron pocket and unlocked it. The apartment was neat as a pin and when Rock walked into the small living room, it was bright and cheery. The large window let the light in and had a view of the tiny, manicured back yard.

The bedroom consisted of a double bed, chest of drawers and a small closet. The kitchen was galley-style with a four burner gas stove and a small refrigerator. The drop-leaf table for two sat across from a cabinet with a stainless steel sink.

Rock was delighted with the place. It was all he needed and more. "It's great!" he enthused. "I know I'll be happy here."

His land-lady smiled broadly at him and said, "I'll be glad to have you, but don't you want to know what the rent is?" Rock dreaded the question; what if he couldn't afford it? "I'll let you have it for two hundred-fifty dollars a month," Beatrice offered.

Rock couldn't believe his lucky streak and said, "I don't have any money until I get my first check, but I can pay you then."

"I thought as much," she said cheerily. "I have no problem with that but in the meantime you can mow my lawn and do odd jobs around here on the weekends."

"It's a deal," Rock agreed not believing his stroke of luck.

"Oh, by the way, to everyone here, I'm Widow Simmons. My husband passed away two years ago. The reason I can charge a little less rent is because he left me well-fixed. I just need people around me; I don't like to be alone and I enjoy the company of my guests."

"When can I move in?"

"Tomorrow will be fine. I know you want to get out of the motel as soon as possible. I'm sure you can't afford to stay there much longer."

"You're right. Thank you."

"I'll let you out then." Before he left, Beatrice looked him over and added, "Don't be offended but my husband was built just like you are and his clothes are still in the closet upstairs. You see, I couldn't bear to get rid of them. I always knew that when the time came, I'd give them to a worthy cause. I think you're it."

Rock lucked out again! The clothes he wore were very dirty and he couldn't wait to get them off. "I'll see you after work. I'll give you some of Ray's clothes to try on then." Rock hugged her impulsively and she shyly smiled in return. "I think we'll get along just fine," she said blushing.

"That was a thank-you hug. I appreciate all you're doing for me."

"You can be the son I never had," she said enthusiastically, "See you tomorrow," and she ushered him through the door.

CHAPTER

The next day after work, Rock moved into his new apartment. He didn't have any belongings except his personal toiletries.

Mrs. Simmons opened the door with a huge smile on her face. "Welcome and come in. Why don't you start with trying on Dan's clothes and then come back down, I have a few surprises for you."

What the heck could it be now? Rock thought. He was curious to find out. "Ok, thanks," he said and took the stairs two at a time. When he opened the door the smell of furniture polish greeted him and the room was clean as a whistle. Rock couldn't help compare the neat little apartment to the barren prison cell he'd occupied for the past ten years.

He put his shaving things in the bathroom, took a much needed shower and decided to try on the pile of clothes lying on the bed. The first two shirts were too tight across the back, but a checkered flannel one, several short-sleeved cotton shirts, t-shirts and a tan jacket fit. There were also two pairs of jeans and some under shorts. Rock was amazed that they all fit. Now he wouldn't have to buy anymore clothes for a while. His money was gone and he wouldn't get paid until the end of the week.

Beatrice knocked at the door. Rock picked up the clothes he couldn't use and gave them to her. "Its high-time I get rid of them," she said. "I'll give them to the church; someone there can use them. By the way, I made a pot of chicken and dumplings so you have something to eat tonight."

Rock's stomach growled. He had survived on the donuts they have at the plant for the last couple of days. "You're so kind; I'll never be able to repay you."

"Just your being here will be enough," Mrs. Simmons replied. "By the way, my name is Beatrice, please call me that. Ma'am won't do, my friends all call me by my first name." She took Rock by the hand. "Come, I have another surprise for you." She led him down the stairs and into the attached garage where a Chrysler roadster sat. It was spit-shine polished. "My Dan took pride in keeping his cars spotless. I've kept it washed in his honor since it was his treasure. I'd like you to have it."

"Oh, I couldn't," Rock protested. "You've done too much for me already!" But he bent over to look inside the car and found it looked as nice inside as out.

"I believe the gas tank is full."

"It's not my business, but when did Dan die?"

Beatrice didn't hesitate, "Two years ago; God rest his soul. Dan was a good man; we were married for fifty wonderful years." Her eyes filled with tears. "His heart attack was sudden and quickly he was gone. I'm just glad he didn't suffer."

Rock hugged her affectionately, "Please don't cry," he said.

Beatrice stiffened and set her jaw. "I must go on. Life is for the living and Don would kick me in the butt if I sat around feeling sorry for myself." She changed the subject, "I have my quilting class this evening so you'll have to eat alone."

"Most days I'll be beat when I get home from work and I'll want to get some shut-eye anyway," he replied. Secretly he hoped she wouldn't expect him to eat with her every night. Rock liked his privacy.

As it turned out he didn't have to worry because she added, "I'll pack you a lunch for tomorrow, but after that sonny, you're on your own," she said and winked at him. "At least you won't have to walk anymore."

"I love you little lady! Thank you."

"Well, I've got things to do," she said and walked to the door.

After she left Rock sat down on the old, mohair couch that had seen better days and turned on the small TV. In minutes he was sound asleep, snoring softly.

The next day, work at the parts factory ended at noon and all the workers got to go home early.

CHAPTER

6

On Friday, Rock received his first paycheck and felt rich. He decided to go to town and purchase some tennis shoes and white socks. He stopped in front of the mercantile store, parking next to the curb and was about to get out of the car when his heart skipped a beat. Ellen was across the street entering a women's shop! The familiar longing for her washed over him, but he quickly quelled the idea because she'd sent him the "Dear John" letter and he didn't know how she'd react. He thought she was the love of his life and wanted her to be again.

Rock knew it wasn't wise but he decided to go to her house to see her soon. When she came out of the store she looked directly at him, but didn't recognize the man in the car. No wonder he thought, he didn't have a beard or mustache when they were together.

Rock couldn't shake the feeling that he urgently had to talk to Ellen. After a week of dreaming of her at night and thinking of her constantly during the day, he decided he wouldn't put it off any longer. When it got dark, he drove down the gravel road that led to her little house, but stopped and parked in some trees a block away.

Ellen's car was in the driveway and a light was on in the kitchen so Rock knew she was home. He peeked into the kitchen window and watched her walk back and forth preparing dinner for herself. Rock thought Ellen looked good enough to eat. She had her thick auburn hair tied back in a pony-tail. Her generous breasts showed through the bulky sweatshirt she wore. God knew he wanted to fondle those tits and hear her moan with pleasure.

Suddenly the screen door opened and Rock ran for cover. Rusty, Ellen's Golden Retriever bounded out the door of the house and stopped in his tacks. He lifted his nose into the air, started barking and ran toward the woods. Rock wanted to run because he was sure the dog sensed he was there. He'd given Rusty to Ellen for Valentine's Day when he was a little pup. He and Rock had developed a special bond before he was thrown in prison. Now, even though he was an old dog he must remember his scent. The closer Rusty got to him the louder he barked.

"Quiet!" Rock whispered loudly, but the dog didn't pay attention. Rock stepped out from behind the trees and Rusty launched himself at Rock knocking him to the ground and smothered him with kisses. Rock hugged the dog fiercely and rubbed his face in the dog's fur.

Then Ellen's voice loudly called Rusty. The dog cocked his head in her direction but didn't move, he just stood in place whining. It hurt Rock to do so, but he stood up and commanded, "Go back, Rusty now!" The dog looked at him with mournful eyes and stood still. "Go!" Rock said sternly and Rusty slowly walked away. He wanted to steal his old buddy and take him home with him but he couldn't.

In the meantime he heard Ellen scolding the animal. "Rusty! Shame on you! You know you shouldn't chase rabbits at night. You're a bad boy. Now get in the house."

Rock felt heartsick as he made his way through the woods to his car. "That didn't go so well," he thought to himself. He was on the verge of tears as he drove twenty miles an hour over the speed limit back to his apartment. I didn't go far enough away he told himself. He knew he'd never leave now that he's seen Ellen and he longed to be with her again.

CHAPTER

Rock thought about how the robbery caper began, playing it over and over in his mind. He and his three buddies played poker in the back room of their favorite watering hole every week.

Rick was assistant manager of the Grand Junction Community Bank. Jason was the baseball coach at Fullerton High School and Sam ran a filling station at the edge of town. They seemed like an odd group but they went to school together. Their friendship lasted long after the school days were behind them.

"Geez," Sam complained, "Since they built the new Amoco Station a block down the street from me, my business is half of what it was. I'm in serious need of some cash."

Rick agreed. "The bank doesn't pay much and I'm struggling to pay back my student loans."

Jason said, "Amen. My wife spends money like I'm a millionaire. I'm in debt up to my Ears. Our credit cards are maxed out and we owe debts all over town. My telephone got shut off last week for non-payment."

"What all you guys complaining about? You know you all over spend your incomes," Rock said.

"Easy for you to say," Rick shouted angrily. "You're a bachelor and only have yourself to worry about!"

"Shut-up Rick! I'm a plumber and and make a decent wage. The only difference between us is that I save some of my money."

The conversation was cut short because no one felt like playing poker any longer. Sam threw his cards on the table and the others also folded. They all walked out of the room without saying another word.

The next week Rock had a call so he was late the poker game. "Hi guys!" he greeted the others. All three nodded but didn't answer him. Rock sat down at the table and waited for one of them to deal the cards. No one did so Rock spoke up, "Ok, let's put last week behind us and forget it ever happened."

"Not a chance!" Sam yelled. "I've been thinking and I want you to listen to the plan I have." Curious, everyone listened to what he had to say.

"I can't wait," Rock said sarcastically.

Sam went on, "I think we should rob Rick's bank and then we'd have plenty of cash."

"Right! And we'll go to jail if we get caught," Jason said emphatically.

"We won't get caught. Rick knows the bank inside out so it would be a walk in the park," Sam spoke up.

"Count me out," Rock exclaimed, standing up to leave.

"Sit down!" Sam ordered. "It's all for one and one for all." The other guys agreed.

Rick said thoughtfully, "It sounds like a plan, let me think about it. I'll let you know next week."

Rock stood up. "You guys are crazy," he said disgustedly. "I'm outta here," and he left the room without looking back.

The following week, Rick reported. "I think I should leave the back unlocked when I leave work and we could enter that door after midnight."

"Isn't there an alarm system?" Jason asked.

"I'll conveniently forget to turn it on," Rick said.

"How do we get into the vault?" Jason asked.

"That would be a problem, I don't know the combination, but I know Jim Edwards does. I also know he's going on vacation next week and as assistant manager he'll have to give me the combo."

"There you go!" Sam said excitedly. "When do you think we should do this?"

"Damn," Rick said, "I forgot about the night guard.

"So, we can take care of him," Sam returned.

"You've got to be kidding. You're talking about hurting a human being."

"Let's forget about the whole thing," Jason stated firmly.

"By the way, where is that chicken Rock tonight?" Sam demanded.

"Maybe he's got a belly ache." Sam laughed.

Suddenly Rick had a change of heart. "He's probably right. Maybe we should just ditch the whole idea," Jason groaned.

"I was already planning what I would do with all that money," Sam added.

"Don't be stupid. The last thing we can do is go on a spending spree. Everyone will wonder why we're suddenly rich."

"Then what good is the money if we can't spend it?" Sam asked with disgust.

"Tonight has gotten us nowhere. Let's take a breather and come up with some new ideas. I'm sure something will come to mind."

CHAPTER

8

His situation was weighing on Rock's mind. His job at the factory and being paid minimum wage couldn't keep him afloat. He had to do something he never thought he would have to do, which was retrieve the money he had kept for a rainy day. Rock justified the idea by telling himself that if this wasn't a rainy day what was?"

He drove to Collins State Park and slowed down near a rock that looked like a loaf of baked bread. Rock got out of the car, popped the trunk and took out a shovel. He walked to the base of the outcrop and began digging. When he saw how close the park's expansion program had come, he feared all was lost, but after close inspection he realized his hiding place was intact.

Rock carried his shovel to the hiding place and dug deep into the spot he thought he'd hid the money. The shovel hit solid rock with a clang. Perplexed, Rock moved over three feet and tried again with the same result.

"Damn It!" he cursed. "Where the Hell is it? I'm sure I buried it here!" After a few more tries Rock hit the jackpot. The burlap bag, although torn and seeped with sand was there in its hiding place. He lifted the heavy bag, lay it down on the ground and checked inside. He grinned when he saw the stacks of bills. This is my way to freedom he thought and he dragged the bag to the car. What should I do with the money he asked himself. Then he answered his own question. He would deposit the money in four different banks under an assumed name.

Feeling on top of the world, Rock drove to his apartment, happier than he'd been in a long time. The money wouldn't erase the ten long years Rock had spent in prison but it certainly would lesson some of his pain.

CHAPTER

9

Ellen was sitting at her office desk at Solar Realty when the phone rang. It was a personal call from her best friend Lucy. She blurted out without saying hello. "Hey," she said excitedly, "Did you know Rock got out a few days ago?"

Ellen's hear raced, "No I didn't," she replied with a shiver running down her spine.

At Ellen's silence, Lucy panicked. "You aren't thinking of seeing him are you?" she screamed.

"I don't know," Ellen replied indecisively.

"Don't start that again! Good God, he's a convicted felon! Besides you broke it off with him. Dan is a great guy and treats you like a queen."

"Gotta go," Ellen said and hung up the phone. Unknown to Ellen, Rock drove by her Real estate office several times, wanting to go in and talk to her. Suddenly he knew that he shouldn't so he drove back to his apartment to make out a list of the men who'd ratted on him and decide how he would get back at them.

Rock sat in a kitchen chair at the table with a pen and paper in front of him. He listed the three men's names and left a space below each one for the method of getting rid of them. He bit down on the end of the pen thinking which man he should begin with.

Since Rock thought Sam was an opinionated big mouth, he would start with him. He thought about the many arguments they'd had and what he could do to eliminate him. Finally, he decided that since Sam was a fishing addict, his accident should occur on the water. He imagined different scenarios but couldn't do them unless someone was with him to help with the deed. But then no one else should know about this, so he will do it by himself. He would have to make sure Sam was dead so he couldn't finger him.

Before he could change his mind Rock opened his cell phone and called Sam's number. After several rings his gruff voice answered. Rock greeted him, "Hey old buddy, its Rock," in a friendly voice.

There was a long silence on the line. "When did you get out?"

"Last week. I thought we could get together, I missed you guys," he lied.

Sam lowered his voice and mumbled, "All of us decided we wouldn't have anything to do with you because you went to prison and all.

"I thought we could drop a line in the river, catch some Redfish." Rock could feel Sam weakening.

"Probably could if we met at the cove where no one will see us.

Rock smiled to himself. "Great! How about Saturday, at six a.m.?"

"Sounds like a plan!"

"Man, I have a favor to ask you. My equipment is too old to use. Do you have any extra that I could use?"

"Sure, I've got at least five poles I can bring and I'll stop and get some bait too."

"Gotta go," Rock said.

"How come?" Sam asked, obviously wanting to talk.

"I've got things to do and people to see."

"What?"

"See yah Saturday, good-bye," Rock said cutting him off and he hung up the phone.

CHAPTER

10

Aforeman from Park Products called Rock on Friday night and asked him if he could work the next day. He had to turn him down with the excuse that he had an appointment. "Damn-it to Hell," Rock thought, he could use the money.

Saturday was a beautiful, warm day with puffy clouds floating in the blue sky. It would be a good day to relax and enjoy but Rock had to put his plan into motion.

It only took ten minutes to drive to the river. Rock was sure to park the car in a copse of trees so anyone parking down the road couldn't see it. Rock locked the car then walked down to the water's edge.

To his surprise Sam was already there but Rock hadn't seen his car anywhere. So he was afraid someone would see his car too. Rock laughed at the thought; he didn't want to be seen with him. What if Sam had a plan to hurt him? He had to stay alert.

Sam looked around when he saw him coming. "There you are," he said while busily tying a sinker on the line of one of the poles.

"Hey yourself," Rock called, "No see for a spell." Rock had to sound pleasant.

Sam ordered, "Make yourself useful!" Rock helped him gather up the fishing supplies then together they made their way to Sam's old wooden boat. The painted skiff was peeling and had seen better days, but the wreck floated like a champion.

The boat leaned slightly to one side when the two men stepped in. "You gained some weight in the last ten years," Rock commented.

"What about it?" Sam asked immediately going on the defensive. In fact the man had gained about thirty pounds, most of it in a huge beer belly that hung over his pants like a sack of flour.

Rock fastened the oars securely to the boat and both men began rowing. "Where are we going?" Rock asked.

"To a special hole I know," Sam answered smugly. For a while neither of them spoke and the only sound was the dip of the oars into the water, rising and falling in rhythm.

"Stop rowing!" Sam ordered. "This is it!" He swung his arm around. "Red fish like to hide in those weeds and the water is about ten feet deep so we don't have to do anything but hang our line over the side of the boat."

Rock started to move the anchor to pitch it over the side of the boat then clutched his shoulder and cried out in pain. Sam looked at him with alarm. "What's wrong?" he hollered.

"It's my shoulder, an old injury I got in basic training. When I lift heavy things my arm goes out of its socket. It hurts like hell," he embellished.

"Let me take care of that," Sam urged, "You sit down."

Rock moved toward the seat, but when Sam hoisted the anchor he grabbed an oar and hit Sam over the head. The blow caused Sam to pitch forward one foot in the boat, the other dangling over the side. Quickly Rock knocked the one in the boat over the side and heaved Sam's body into the water. He hit the water hard and immediately began floundering, waving his arms frantically.

"I can't swim!" he cried, "Help me!" Rock looked at him with distaste and took the oar and smacked Sam over the head. The man's body sank and some bubbles rose to the surface of the water. Suddenly the body surfaced but Sam didn't move. To be sure Sam was dead, Rock rowed over him and stopped in the water, right on top of him and stayed there until he was sure the life was sucked out of Sam's body.

Then he rowed back to shore. When he looked at the water, nothing could be seen. The surface was calm like a mirror. Rock arranged the bucket and extra poles in the boat and threw one out in the water. Satisfied, he stepped out on the ground and walked away without looking back.

He made his way to his car and drove swiftly back to the main road. Suddenly he began to shake, it was a delayed reaction. He had actually murdered a man! Rock felt so sick to his stomach he almost stopped on the side of the road to throw up, but pulled himself together. I've got to go back to the apartment he thought and hide the money. It wasn't safe in its hiding place under the bed.

By the time he got back to the apartment he knew what to do. He would rearrange his closet so no one would find lit. When Rock saw the other cars in the driveway, he remembered it was Beatrice's day to host her quilting bee. He parked on the street and entered the door, ready to hurry up the stairs, but Mrs. Simmons stopped him. "Are you Ok?" she asked sounding concerned.

"I feel a little nauseated; I probably just picked up a bug."

"Poor boy, go upstairs and rest, after while I'll bring you a bowl of soup." The women had stopped their quilting and were watching the scene with interest. When Beatrice entered the room, one woman asked, "Who was that? He looks familiar."

"My new renter," Bea replied.

"I think I know him too," another woman said, "But he has a mustache and beard now."

"Oh stop you old gossips!" Beatrice admonished.

But one of the women insisted, "He looks like that Rock guy that just got released from prison!"

Beatrice's face went pale but she hurried into the kitchen to prepare a tray of cookies and iced tea to provide the women the snack that was expected. After everyone was finished eating the women left. Beatrice sat down in her chair thinking, was it true? Rock was an ideal renter, but what did she know about his past? At the very least she would have to ask him, she thought.

Meanwhile, Rock had hauled the money out from under the bed and put the bag in the closet. Then he took the spare blankets and sheets off the top shelf and placed them on the floor. On the top shelf he placed a pile of shorts and socks and his several pair of shoes. Rock arranged his hanging clothes on hangers then looked at his handiwork. No one would ever see the bag or look there, not even his land lady. Rock didn't think she was nosey, but he didn't know for sure.

After he was finished, he warmed up a cup of coffee, drank it down and nearly spit it out. His stomach was upset over his actions that day. He hoped Sam's body wouldn't be found not even though no one would think he was responsible. Feeling marginally better, he lay down on the bed and fell asleep.

Mrs. Simmons brought up his soup but didn't wake him. I'll talk to him later, she thought. Right now he didn't feel well and sleep was what he needed.

CHAPTER

11

Ellen twirled the silver friendship/engagement ring on her finger. She had been dating Ken for a quite some time now and she knew he was serious about her. The feeling wasn't mutual.

Although she had broken off her relationship with Rock years ago, she didn't think she could forget him. Now that he was out of prison she wanted to see him again.

When Ken came over to pick her up to go to a movie, Ellen faked sickness and sent him on his way.

Anyone would like him because he was a great guy, but she knew he wasn't for her. In all fairness she'd break up with him and give his ring back.

CHAPTER

12

Although Rock had to go to see his parole officer every month, he hated it because he thought the man had decided he was guilty. Besides that, he was convinced Rock was a drug addict and made him pee in a cup after every session. However he had to admit that Rock was the most honest of the felons he'd handled. He was never late for his appointments and paid his maintenance fees every time he came in.

Although he'd never let on to Rock he believed his stint in prison had straightened him out. Rock had showed him the stub from a check from Park Products. The factory was highly regarded and didn't hire anyone who had a bad attitude. He'd like to check up on Rock, see what he'd done before. An application helped somebody understand a person. For kicks he'd ask Bud Riley a man he knew well and was in charge of employment at the factory.

Beatrice met Rock at the door and invited him in. The last thing he wanted to do was have a chat with the lady, but because he knew she was lonely he did as she asked.

When he was settled in, she brought him a cup of black tea. Rock thanked her profusely and accepted the cup, but in truth he hated tea.

Beatrice sat down opposite him and looked him in the eye. Without preamble she blurted, "Are you a con man?" she asked him.

Rock could tell by her tone she didn't believe it but wanted to be sure. Rock cleared his throat and put on an innocent face. "Of course not!" he exclaimed. "Whatever made you think that?"

Beatrice didn't know how to answer him, but after a moment of silence she replied, "By the grapevine."

It was just what Rock was afraid of; the gossip about him was beginning. "Look, I'm from Pittsburgh, PA and worked in a steel factory for five years. I got sick of it and came down here where the summers are longer."

Beatrice looked relieved. "I shouldn't have asked you because my instincts are always right. I'm sorry son, I won't embarrass you again."

Rock gave her a hug and hurried up to his little apartment, took off his shoes and collapsed on the bed fully dressed. It had been a long day.

CHAPTER

13

The next day after work Rock was determined to put his fears behind him and go to see the lovely Ellen. He could think of nothing else and he had to find how she felt one way or the other.

Boldly he parked in her driveway and walked up to the front door. He found it unlocked, so he went in without knocking.

Ellen heard the door open and came running from the kitchen to see who it was. When she saw Rock standing there she stopped in her tracks, stared at him, her lips moved but no sound came out.

Slowly Rock walked over to her, took her in his arms and hugged her close to him. At first she stiffened but when Rock started kissing her neck she leaned into him. "I missed you so much," Rock whispered in her ear.

A tear slid down her cheek and she whispered back, "I missed you too."

Rock pushed her away and said firmly, "We have to talk. I want to clear the air between us." Ellen nodded and together the two of them walked slowly to the sofa. When they were settled, Rock looked into Ellen's big, blue eyes and began, "I'm not guilty; you know that don't you?"

Ellen dropped her eyelids and looked down at her lap, then raised her head and got lost in his warm, brown eyes. "I always believed in you," she said softly.

Rock took her hand and gently kissed her palm. "I know you did," he answered. "They lied to the cops and I took the rap."

"Even though everyone else thought you were guilty, I never thought you were."

"Let me tell you the whole story. You are a good listener, but don't condemn me until you hear all that I have to say." Ellen shook her head no but Rock started to speak. "You know I play poker every week with Rick, Jason and Sam." Ellen nodded. "We always talked about women like guys do, but one night the subject changed. I'm the only single man so I didn't take part in the conversation. Suddenly all of them told their sad story and it seems they all were broke for different reasons and needed help. What started as a joke turned real. Sam talked about robbing Rick's bank with his inside help. The next week the talk grew serious and they began to plan how they could pull it off. I walked out angry. No way was I going to be part of their hair-brained scheme. Before I left I warned them that such a caper could land them in prison for a long time. Everyone was sure they had the perfect plan and never would get caught. I tried to tell them different, but they wouldn't listen. Sam was particularly adamant about it so I was disgusted with him; we were always at odds about everything. Rick was different. I could tell he wanted no part of the deal either but he didn't speak up. Jason has always been a guy that won't take a side in any disagreement but felt the robbery would be a lark and the whole thing would never materialize."

Ellen stood up. "I'm going to get a bottle of wine," she said. "I feel like this conversation will go on for a while." She left the room and brought back a bottle of Merlot and two glasses. After pouring the wine she handed one to Rock, sat down and said, "Go on."

Rock anxiously began to talk again. "I skipped the next week and didn't play poker. However, the guys wouldn't leave me alone. They said if I didn't help them they were convinced I would rat them out. In the end they squealed on me and I took the rap. I'm going to get revenge if it's the last thing I do!" Rock stated bitterly.

Ellen put her hand over Rocks and squeezed it. "You can't Rock," she cried. "Don't lower yourself to their standards."

Rock knew she was right but the desire to make them pay was too strong. "I have to do it," he said angrily. He looked intently at Ellen. "Do you want to hear the rest of the story or not?"

"Go ahead," she murmured quietly.

Rock drained his glass of wine and held it out for a refill. When Ellen had filled it, he began talking again. "Since Rick wouldn't go along with the plan, Sam and Jason devised another plan. An armored truck came to the bank every morning and they devised a plan to rob it and get rich in the process. When they told me about their plan I flatly refused to go along with it. But to make a long story short, they held something over my head and vowed to make it public."

"What?" Ellen asked.

Rock brushed her off, "That's immaterial. It happened a long time ago." He asked for one more refill of wine and after he drank it he spoke a little bit slower and with a bit of a lisp. "Because I didn't want that story to come out I agreed to drive the get-away car."

"That makes you an accessory to the crime!" Ellen objected.

"I realize that is true, but now I've paid the price and the other guys haven't."

"Forget it; go on with your life."

"I can't. The bitterness burns my insides and besides I've already started my pay backs."

Ellen was horrified. "What have you done?" she asked panicking.

"You'll know soon enough," Rock said contritely. "Look, I'd better leave now. I've missed you so much and I wanted to hold you, but it didn't turn out that way. Good-bye my love," Rock said sorrowfully and left her before he started to cry.

The next morning Sam's death made the headlines in the local paper. Rock read the story with deep regret. Why did he do such a thing? He was not a murderer. He deserved to go back to prison but shuddered at the thought. He hoped Ellen wouldn't go to the authorities. He never should have told anyone he realized too late.

Although Rock seldom drank, he stopped at the 'Do Drop In' to drown his sorrows. He drank enough beer to get falling-down drunk. The mood toward him was cold, even people he knew shied away from him. He was about to leave when Rick walked in. Rock dropped his head and stared at the bar. To Rock's surprise Rick walked over and slapped him on the shoulder. "Why didn't you tell me you were out?" he asked.

"You know I took the rap for you, why would I call?"

"I wasn't part of that; ratting you out I mean."

"Yeah, of course you weren't," Rock answered sarcastically. "You know you guys ruined my life don't you? No one will hire a con."

"Think this over. I didn't want to go along with it, you know that don't you?" Rock thought he was telling the truth but he wouldn't let him know that.

"Too bad Sam drowned isn't it?" Rick said looking into Rock's eyes. "You didn't have anything to do with that, did you?"

"I admit we didn't get along but I would never do something to hurt him."

"If you say so," Rick replied doubtfully as he stared at Rock then walked out the door.

Rock shouldn't have been driving but he made it back without any problem.

Beatrice met him at the door and looked him over with distaste. She realized he was drunk and yelled, "You're drunk!"

"I'm sorry," Rick lied.

"I don't rent to alcoholics," she said stiffly.

"I'm sorry," Rock said again. ""For your penance you will go to church with me next Sunday. Don't shake your head no. If you want to stay here you'll do as I say. Now get upstairs and sleep it off. When you wake up you'll have a horrible thirst. I'll see that you get some orange juice. Now git!"

Rock hurried up the stairs. She sounds like my mother, "I'm a grown man and I don't need a lecture." He got as far as the sofa, sat down with a thud and closed his eyes.

He woke up a few hours later to grab his cell phone when it rang but dropped it on the floor. After he picked it up, he growled, "Hey."

Jason laughed into his ear. "Rick told me you're back in town. What you say we get together and play some poker?"

"Not on your life," Rock returned.

"Don't hold a grudge. What's done is done."

"I lost ten years of my life because of you assholes. I'll never forgive you!"

"If that's the way you feel, I say to Hell with you," Jason hollered and snapped his phone shut. At least he didn't mention Sam's death, Rock thought.

He shuffled into the kitchen and found the bottle of OJ in the refrigerator. Beatrice had been true to her word. Then he thought, "What the hell, she must have a key. Maybe it's time I flew this coop."

CHAPTER

14

Ken was persistent. He called Ellen every day, sometimes several times a day. If she wasn't home, he left a message.

Ellen was tougher than nails and swore like a trooper even though she didn't do it until she was really irritated. She called Ken's number and when he answered she shouted, "Stop calling me! We need to talk face to face. I'll give you a half an hour to get here or I'm reporting you for harassment!" She sat to wait for him, knowing he'd be there without a doubt.

Within fifteen minutes Ken knocked loudly on her door. "Open up," he shouted.

Ellen made him stand there for at least ten minutes while he lay on the buzzer. She threw the door open and said coldly, "Do come in before you wear out my doorbell."

After sitting down, Ken patted the sofa next to him and said, "Come on honey."

Ellen gave him a look, "No!" she said firmly. "Listen Ken, you have been smothering me. I like my independence. I've been giving our relationship a lot of thought and we aren't meant to be together." She took off the friendship ring and tossed it to him.

"I know what this is all about," Ken said angrily, "You're seeing that jail-bird, aren't you?"

"I've heard he's out of jail but I haven't seen him," she lied.

"You don't lie very well, sweetheart, but I know when I'm not wanted." Ken got up from the sofa and nearly stumbled over his own feet.

Ellen had to stifle a laugh, "Watch out!" she said and smiled at him.

"Don't flash those dimples at me." Then he held out the ring and said, "I know a lot of girls who would like to have this."

"There's no sense in our arguing. I think you should leave now," Ellen instructed.

"I'm on my way," he said as he hurried to the door. "You're such a bitch," he called over his shoulder as he left.

Ellen sat in the chair and asked herself, "Dear God, what have I done? If Rock won't have me, I'll probably end up an old maid," she said as she stared off into space for a long while. "Oh well, tomorrow is the first day of my new life and I'm going to make the best of it!" she chimed.

CHAPTER

15

Examination of the soil along the boat ramp indicated there were two men near Sam's boat. Suddenly the investigator's thoughts changed direction. The authorities concluded that Sam's drowning was suspicious.

Crime scene investigators measured each footprint. There were two different ones, with the larger one being a size twelve which was Sam's shoe size. The other prints were a size nine which meant that they belonged to a small person and that particular pattern was that of a navy blue Nike tennis shoe which was sold in every sporting goods store in the area.

Rock was nervous when he read the article in the newspaper. He had to get rid of those shoes quick! He grabbed them out of the closet and looked them over. The canvas had shrunk from being in the water. Panicking, Rock put them in a paper bag and drove to a trash compactor five miles away and threw them in, making sure they were on the bottom of the container covered with other garbage. Satisfied the shoes would not be found before the garbage truck came on Monday. He whistled as he drove back to his apartment.

Rock made himself a grilled cheese sandwich for lunch, feeling secure and on top of the world. It was a close call but he had taken care of it.

CHAPTER

16

Beatrice's friend Millie called her to report all the gossip she'd heard through the week. Most of the time Bea tuned Millie out because she didn't know half of the people Millie was chattering about, but her ears perked up when she started on Rock. Without thinking, Beatrice spilled the beans about his coming home drunk.

"You should get rid of him," Millie told her. Before you know it, he'll attack you."

"You're nuts, you old bag. He's young enough to be my son!"

"Any woman is fair game for a man. Did you ever find out any more about him? You could have a murderer in your house."

"That's enough! I'm hanging up. I have better things to do than listen to your gossip."

"Well, I never...." Millie said and also hung up.

Beatrice turned on the television and sat down to watch her soap operas. When she heard Rock come home from work she didn't greet him like she always did. Milles's words still rankled and no matter how she tried she couldn't forget them. Maybe she should call that Kurtz guy who was a computer geek and ask him to check Rock out. Yes, that's a good idea, she thought. She was confident she'd prove Millie wrong.

In a few days, Lyle Kurtz came over to see Beatrice. She gave him a friendly smile but he didn't return it. Instead he slowly handed her a piece of typed paper. She scanned it and Bea's hand flew to her mouth.

"My God!" she cried and began to shake with dread washing over her. In her haste to rent the apartment she had mistakenly rented it to a con. I must evict him immediately! she thought; but what if he refused to go?

Beatrice waited for Rock to come home from work and asked him to come in. He didn't think anything of it because she often asked him in for an assortment of reasons. She's just lonely, Rock told himself and sat down in a familiar chair. It was then he noticed her nervousness.

Finally she spoke. "I have bad news," she started, wringing her hands. "I must ask you to leave."

"Rock's face went white, "Why on earth? Why? What have I done?" he asked.

In spite of herself, Beatrice felt sorry for him so she made up a lie. "My Granddaughter just graduated from college and because she is estranged from her parents, she wants to stay with me until she finds a job and another place to live."

That wasn't the reason Rock knew; somehow his identity had gotten to her and she was afraid of him. He got up determined to take the news in stride. "I'm sorry to hear that, I am very fond of you and hate to leave." Inside he was devastated; where could he go that his past wouldn't haunt him? Everyone condemned him as though he had committed the crime. "Will you give me a week to find another place to live?" Rock asked hopelessly.

"Of course," she answered. "I will also give you a good reference."

Rock doubted that but said, "I'd appreciated it. Do you know of any place I could rent?"

Beatrice knew of one place available but the people would never rent to him when they heard what she'd had to say. "No I don't," she replied convincing herself she was only telling a white lie.

"I'll be leaving then," Rock said and walked to the door. "I'll try to leave as soon as possible," he said coldly and left without saying good-bye.

CHAPTER

17

Rock disguised his voice and made an anonymous call to the Sheriff's department. He asked for Chief Parsons but he was told he was out of the office. Then he asked to talk to the detective on duty. There was a long wait but then a male voice came on the line. "Murphy here," he said.

"I have a tip for you, "Rock said in his disguised voice.

"What?" Murphy asked suspiciously.

"About the Sam Smith case; I know of a man who knows Sam and wears size nine tennis shoes and buys them at Johnson's shoe store. It would behoove you to check it out."

The station had a lot of tips called in but they hadn't amounted to anything. Somehow this one rang true. "Where did you get this information?"

"I shop there too," Rock replied and hung up. He smiled because he'd led the cops on a wild goose chase.

Detective Murphy told the chief about the call he'd received and he told him to follow up on it at once. He jumped into an unmarked car and drove out to Johnson's shoe store.

An elderly man behind the counter looked at his uniform wondering why he was there. "How can I help you?" he asked.

"I'm looking for a man who purchased a pair of size nine, blue Nike tennis shoes."

"Let me check my sales receipts," the clerk replied nervously. He looked back through ten weeks of records and shook his head no. "I'm sorry we didn't sell any of that type of shoe matching that description in the past month."

"Then look further," the detective ordered.

The man sighed but did as Murphy had asked. Finally he found something of interest. "Two months ago we sold a pair of those tennis shoes."

"Let me see it," Murphy said. "Do you know who purchased them?" he asked.

The clerk didn't want to reveal the name of a good customer but answered, "Sure, it's Joe Higgins. He buys all of his shoes here. We give him a discount."

"Where does he live?"

"At Wilson's apartments, a few blocks from here."

"Thank you Sir," the officer said. "You've been a great help," and he hurried out the door. When he got to the car, he radioed the chief, and told him he had a lead. "I'm checking it out."

"Go get him Murphy. It's about time we got lucky!" the chief enthused.

"Ten-four," the detective said, his intuition told him he'd hit pay-dirt.

The super at Wilson's apartments was congenial when detective Murphy showed him his badge.

"We're looking for a Mr. Higgins; what number is his apartment?"

The man hesitated, "Usually Higgins would be at work but he's taking a sick day. He's down in bed with a horrible cold."

"I have to talk to him today," Murphy answered.

The super shrugged, "If you must." He led Murphy to twenty-one A, and left him at the door.

The detective pounded loudly on the door. When there was no answer, he pounded even louder.

The door opened slowly and a very sick man with a red, dripping nose stood there with a fist full of Kleenex. "What do you want?" he asked eyeing Murphy suspiciously.

Again the detective showed his badge.

"Come in then, but it's at your own risk, there are probably germs everywhere."

Murphy had a pneumonia shot last month so he wasn't worried. He walked into the room and looked around; it was neat but there was a rumpled blanket on the couch and the small TV was on.

"Sit down," Joe said between sneezes. "What do you want?" Murphy didn't hesitate because he wanted to get out of there as soon as possible.

"I want to see the tennis shoes you purchased at Johnsons Shoe Store."

"Why?" the man said sniffling.

"Just get them," Murphy ordered.

Joe shuffled off and came back with a shoe box. He removed the cover and took out a pair of brand spanking new tennis shoes. They fit the description but obviously they hadn't been worn.

"Why haven't you worn these?" Murphy asked confounded.

"Haven't had the opportunity; I wear them to play in a senior basketball league but I haven't felt good enough to play." He added with conviction, "It's tough to get old."

"Yep," Murphy added. "I'm sorry to have bothered you, "Go back to bed." And as an afterthought he added, "Get well soon."

When the detective got back to the station he went directly to the chief's office who looked at Murphy expectantly. "What?" he asked, hoping for good news.

"Sorry, chief," Murphy said contritely. "Dead end again."

"Shit!" the chief declared and put his head in his hands. "I want to solve this case so bad I can taste it. Get out of here, and put your thinking cap on again."

CHAPTER

18

At Park Products, Rock was reprimanded for his slacking job performance because he wasn't producing enough. He knew the reason for it was that he wasn't getting enough sleep. For a week now he'd been sleeping in his car. Actually he was living in his car because he couldn't find anyone that would rent to him.

The trunk was filled with his clothes which were all wrinkled and Rock hadn't showered in a week. He had made do, by washing up in the Welcome Center but the woman there was getting suspicious of him.

He decided he would have to call Ellen and beg to crash there until he figured out what he could do. When he called her and told her his circumstances, luckily she felt sorry for him and said he could stay with her until he had another plan.

Thankful for her, he drove to the little cottage. When he got out of the car Ellen and Rusty ran to greet him. "My God, you look awful," she cried. Rock was overcome by the sight of them, it was like coming home. "Don't worry," Ellen said, "We'll get everything sorted out together." Rock followed them into the house and flopped on the sofa, where he was asleep in minutes.

Two hours later when Rock woke up, he went to the bathroom and took a shower. For fifteen minutes he let the warm water sluice over his body until it turned cold. He got out, wiped his body dry and put on the terrycloth robe that was hanging on the back of the door. Rock was too exhausted to do anything even though he felt great from the shower. He wanted to go back to sleep but thought he should spend some time with Ellen.

When he walked down the stairs and into the kitchen, he saw Ellen serving up food onto two plates. "Hello fella," she joked, "What are you doing here?"

"I just stopped by to visit awhile for old time's sake," Rock said grinning.

"I didn't have much in the refrigerator but I figured you needed something to eat." Rock sat down at the table and she put a plate in front of him. He saw that it was filled with a pasta and shrimp salad with a sliced ham sandwich on rye bread.

"It looks wonderful," he told her.

"Tomorrow I'll go grocery shopping and then I'll make you a real meal in the crock pot. I have to make a living you know."

"Can't you take a day off?"

Ellen made a face. "Nope, I've got a good sale to close tomorrow, but I should be home by three o'clock."

"I guess I'll just have to entertain myself then, Rusty won't mind some company. Do you have a good book?"

"I just read one by James Patterson; I know you'd like it."

Rock thought he was enjoying himself so much that he could really get used to it again. It was too bad he only had this long weekend off before he had to go back to work.

Ellen got up and opened the refrigerator, "We're having graham cracker dessert, I remember it's your favorite." That was too much. He got up and threw his arms around her. She ruffled his hair then pulled away. "Don't Rock," she said, "I'm not ready for that yet." Rock's heart lurched when he heard the word "yet" but he decided he wouldn't push her.

That night Ellen made up the sofa for him. She noted the disappointment in his eyes and shook her finger at him and said, "You'll sleep better alone. See you in the morning." She climbed the stairs and was gone.

Rock tossed and turned all night, not able to sleep a wink. What an asshole I am, he thought. Why did I think I could just walk in, and continue what we had before?

After two days of lying around, the walls were closing in on Rock. He walked Rusty each day until the old dog tired then he took a nap with the dog beside him.

Rock needed to get back to work and was glad the weekend was almost over-with as he needed to keep busy. His job was boring but he thought no one else would hire him. He thought about moving on but couldn't bring himself to leave.

CHAPTER

19

Rock began checking the morning newspaper every day. He'd keep looking for another job while he was staying with Ellen knowing he couldn't stay there forever.

One morning he was sitting at the kitchen table drinking coffee and looking at the help wanted section when an ad caught his eye. It read: Experienced Plumber wanted, excellent pay. Call R. J. Richards @ 567-726-8129. Before he could think about it, he flipped open his cell phone and punched in the number.

When a woman answered, he almost hung up but he asked for the person who did the hiring. In a few minutes a man's voice came on the line. "This is Charlie," he said in an authoritative voice.

"I'm inquiring about your ad in the paper for an experienced plumber," Rock said.

"How many years have you worked as a master plumber?" Charlie asked him.

"Since I was twenty years old, and now I'm forty."

"Congrats! Where did you work?"

Rock recited all the false information that he'd put on the Park Products application and then said that he worked in Pittsburgh, PA.

"Sounds like you're a reliable worker. Why don't you come in tomorrow at about one o'clock in the afternoon? I'll be here to interview you personally. Just ask for Charlie James."

"Thank you, Sir," Rock said politely. He was so excited that he called Ellen at work and told her the good news.

"That's wonderful Rock!" she exclaimed, "But I'm busy now, I'll talk to you when I get home."

Rock was deflated by her response but he'd be damned if it would get him down. He considered going to some watering hole but didn't want to be recognized. Instead he took Rusty for a run to let off some steam.

When Rock got back home he looked in the bathroom to see if by chance Ellen had any of her hair color under the sink. He hit the jackpot when he found an unopened box of Nice 'n Easy. After reading the directions he realized it would only take him an hour to transform his appearance.

When he became a black haired man, Rock was sure no one would recognize him. Naturally, he was a graying blonde, then auburn as his disguise. Now he would be something completely different. He wanted to call Ellen and ask her to pick up some brown contacts but he nixed the idea, knowing his eyes would have to be measured.

When Ellen hung up the phone she saw Lucy hurrying toward her. Ellen waived at her and waited for her to approach her desk. "Want to do lunch?" Lucy asked.

"I shouldn't," Ellen replied, "I just got finished with a closing and I have another one at four o'clock."

"Come on sister, I ain't seen you for a long time," Lucy said in her best Humphrey Bogart imitation.

Ellen couldn't help but laugh. "Ok you're on," she said and picked up her purse.

"Chong's Chinese, I hope."

"What else?" Lucy said and the two friends linked arms and left the building. They were half way through their lunch when Lucy's conversation turned to Rock. "I'm sure you aren't seeing Rock. His old landlord and her old-crony friends are gossiping galore and the news about him is the talk of the town."

Ellen fought to compose herself, "What do you mean?" she asked.

"The word is that he got drunk every night and she had to evict him because he tried sneaking women up to his apartment." Ellen gulped then sneezed to cover-up her reaction.

Lucy wasn't fooled, she looked at Ellen suspiciously. "What's the matter with you? Don't you like people talking about your old squeeze?"

"Leave it alone!" Ellen cried and noticed that many of the customers were staring at her. She stood up from the table, looked at them and shouted, "Go to Hell!" and ran out the door.

The heat of the day enveloped Ellen as she ran to her car sobbing. She could hear Lucy calling her name but didn't look back at the restaurant. She dialed her assistant at the office and told her to take over, then drove home.

Thankfully, Rock's car was in the driveway. She hoped he would finally make love to her that night. Ellen let out a scream when she entered the house and saw a black haired man coming in the back door. "What's wrong? Why are you home early?" Rock yelled to her.

Ellen began sobbing out of control, "I'm sorry," she wailed. "For a minute I thought you were a stranger." She ran to the stairs and hurried up to her room. Rock tried to catch her but she moved too quickly. He heard the bedroom door slam so he knew going after her was futile. He sat down on a lower step in frustration; he'd never seen Ellen like this before.

He'd have to wait, give her some time to settle down. He was sure she would tell him the whole story. Rusty padded over to Rock and placed his head in his lap. He could tell by the look in the animal's eyes that he didn't know what was happening either. Rock stood up, "Come on old buddy, I'll feed you and have a bite myself because it looks like there won't be any cooking here tonight."

CHAPTER

20

When Rock pulled into Richard's Plumbing there were several trucks in the lot, loading on or loading off supplies for jobs.

When he entered the building, a tall man with a large beer belly met him. He had dark circles under his eyes, a pot-marked complexion and a red nose, usually indicating a heavy drinker.

The man looked Rock over, noting his blue jeans and flannel shirt. Well, he's ready for work he thought. "You must be Rock," he said. "All ready to go to work I see."

"I sure am Sir."

"Call me Charlie, everyone else does."

"What do you want me to do?"

"Another plumber is here and ready to go on a call. His name is Walt, you can ride with him. Your pay will depend on how you handle the call. We always ask the customers about your performance so be sure you do it right the first time."

The other guy was tall and muscular. He and Rock looked like they could be brothers. He had rugged good looks with black hair and eyes which was the only difference between them. Rock's eyes were hazel, and he was younger looking.

"Come on," he said, "A toilet is clogged up and we'd better get to it." They both hopped into a new Ford pick-up truck with the name, 'J.R. Richards Plumbing Company' painted on the side doors.

"This old lady always has something wrong," Walt said.

"How so?"

"I think she's lonely and wants some company."

They pulled up to a gray house with a picket fence around it. An elderly, white-haired woman saw them coming and opened the door. Rock took one look at her and wanted to run. She was one of the women in Beatrice's quilting bee. He tried to make an excuse not to go in, but Walt looked at him strangely. "Why?" he asked.

Rock couldn't think of anything to say so he told the truth. "She's the friend of an old land-lady of mine and the biggest gossip in town. She spread the word that I was a drunk and a womanizer."

"Wow! I'd go in alone, but she's spotted you so…."

"I'll face the music then, but I hope I don't lose my temper."

"You'd better not or you'll be out of work tomorrow. You really don't want to mess with Charlie."

Rock pulled his visor cap down over his face as far as he could but it really didn't disguise him. Maybe the black hair would do the trick he hoped. The old lady looked them over. Without preamble she snapped, "You look like some scoundrel I know but you have black hair."

Walt saved the day, "He's my brother," he said firmly.

When they inspected the supposedly clogged toilet, all Rock had to do was plunge it, then flush it and the water went down into the trap. Walt clapped his hands. "All done Mrs. Jones; that will be twenty-five dollars please."

"You guys are highway robbers. No wonder your boss is rich. I'll spread the word and no one will call you." She laughed loudly as she came into the room with some moldy looking bills. "Now that you're paid; get out of here. I'll call your boss and tell him that's the last time I'll call him."

Walt and Rock left there quickly, leaving rubber in her driveway when they squealed out. "What a bitch," Walt exclaimed, "Charlie will probably give us a raise when he hears about it!"

After Rock had worked a week, Charlie called him into his office. "Please sit down," he said in a nonchalant voice. What's up? Rock wondered. He sat down and looked at his boss expectantly. Charlie placed a paper on the desk in front of him. "Do you know anything about this?" Rock shook his head no. "I'll have you know that this is the reply from the place that you claimed to have worked at for five years. They deny knowing anyone by your name." Rock shrugged. What a fool he was, he thought. He should have known a company as large as this one would do things by the book.

"I did that because I needed a job badly, but I want you to know my father was a plumber and I went on his calls with him from the time I was ten years old," Rock explained.

"I understand that because Walt reported that you are very competent. However, I felt I should know you from the first time I laid eyes on you. I'm just nosey enough to check you out. What do you think I found out?"

Rock looked at the floor because he knew what it was. "I guess you're going to fire me then." He stood up to leave.

"Wait a minute, come back here. I'll tell you a little secret. I spent some time in jail too; it was only for six months for a lesser crime. Believe me, it was no picnic but you've paid your dues. I don't see why you can't stay on with." He winked at Rock, "Besides, there's no money to steal around here. We work for every cent."

"I appreciate your understanding but I want you to know I was framed. All I can think of is paying back the guys that screwed me."

"Forget that Rock. Get on with your life as best you can. You don't want to end up back in the pen again do you?"

"Nope." However, the look on Rock's face told his boss that he wouldn't forget.

"Forgive but don't forget," Charlie said. "That's the rule."

"I'll keep what you've told me in mind," Rock replied as he walked angrily out the door. Charlie watched him go and wondered how long it would be before Rock was back in prison. Not long, he wagered.

CHAPTER

21

When Rock drove home from work, he saw a football team practicing on a field outside of the high-school. He stopped the car and watched them. He'd played football all four years of high school, as a starting linebacker. When he didn't get the scholarship to Minnesota State U, after attending the tech, he went into the plumbing business with his father.

Rock saw one boy standing alone. On impulse, he got out of the car and approached him. "Wanna throw a couple balls?" he asked him.

"Sure thing! I only play second string, so I don't see much action." The two of them tossed the ball back and forth several times then they began to throw it a little harder and faster. Rock missed one and it came close to where some of the other players were practicing. He ran onto the field and scooped up the ball. Before he could give it back to the young man he was playing with, a hand hit him hard on the shoulder from behind, almost knocking him down.

Rock spun around furious, ready to smack whoever did it. To his surprise he came face to face with Jason. He looked at Rock oddly then recovered and said, "No one is allowed on the field," He stopped talking and looked Rock over again. "It's you, isn't it?" he sneered. "Even with your disguise, I'd know you anywhere, you son-of-a-bitch."

Rock was fuming and wanted to punch his lights out but Jason stood a foot taller than he did and was forty pounds heavier with a neck as wide as a barn door.

"I heard you were out but I thought you'd stay away from me, you little pip-squeak."

Rock curtailed his rage and turned to walk away, his mouth clinched shut and his knees were weak. Don't bully me you asshole, I know just how to pay you back, he thought. He sat in the car for a few minutes to cool down.

His thoughts were of Ellen, their past love and hot sex. He started the car and quickly drove to her cottage. Tonight's the night he thought.

When Rock walked into the house, Ellen was already in her nightie and he whistled when he saw her. Her luscious breasts were barely covered by the lace bodice. "You look hot, babe!" he said with a smile.

"Whoa honey, not tonight, I've got stomach cramps. I think it's that time of the month." Rock wanted to throw her on the sofa and make love to her until she screamed. But when she told him she was only going to eat a little of the casserole and then go to bed, it turned him off.

That night he slept on the sofa again. Disgusted, he told himself that this shit had to stop. Ten years plus is too damn long to be celibate. He was bursting at the seams and he didn't want anyone except Ellen but if this went on much longer he'd take his dick to town, down to Pearl's house of ill-repute.

22

Ellen left earlier since she had to work earlier than Rock did. They hadn't spoken for two days and he was tired of talking to the dog.

When he picked up the paper, the headlines hit him hard. It read "High School Coach Killed in Car Crash." The article described the graphic details of how Jason Baker's car hit a concrete culvert, flew into the air and landed upside down in some trees. When he was pulled from the wreckage he was unrecognizable. It read that the funeral arrangements would be announced later.

Rock's heart beat uncontrollably. He'd lost his temper, thinking that after all his planning how to kill him, he'd been robbed of the satisfaction. "God-damn-it to hell," he swore and threw the paper across the room.

Suddenly he needed to get out of there. He'd go down to the diner for coffee even though people seemed to still recognize him whether his hair was black or not.

Rock was quiet for several days after, appearing to be in deep thought. He didn't tell any jokes or smile anymore and the guys at work wondered what was wrong with him.

Of course Ellen tried to entice him because she was in that frame of mind and he coldly shut her out. Finally his frustration surfaced. He grabbed her by the arm, took her upstairs to the bedroom and threw her on the bed. He unzipped his pants and pulled off her panties. Rock was wild, thrusting into her over and over again until she cried out in pain. He climaxed and rolled off her. Ellen was sobbing uncontrollably.

Rock left the room to take a shower, but when he got there his legs were so weak, he couldn't stand. He clutched for the sink to try to stop his fall, but fell hard on the tile. Rock didn't wonder what was wrong with him, he knew. Prison had changed him. He was bitter and frustrated and worst of all he had just taken it all out on his sweet Ellen.

Rock heard her stir in the bedroom so he hurried down the stairs to avoid her. He was ashamed that he had let the prison poison his mind and plot the deaths of others.

Suddenly Rock thought about the money. My God, I don't have it anymore! He had left it at Beatrice's place! What should he do now? Was it gone? In spite of himself, he wanted that dirty money. One thing for sure, he had to find out where it was. He put his thoughts aside when he heard Ellen coming down the stairs.

Rock couldn't face her because he felt so terrible that he had become the miserable human being he was now.

The door slammed as Ellen left without a word. Within fifteen minutes she was back. "I can't go to work today," she cried and ran up the stairs.

Rock drank a cup of coffee and tried to calm himself down. The robbery that started all this played over and over in his mind. Jason and Sam had attacked the driver at his last stop, tied him up and threw him in the back of the truck. Sam put on the man's uniform and drove the truck to the Community Bank to pick up the money that they were to split.

At that point, Rock pulled up to the curb and they shoved the three large bags filled with money into the trunk of his car, and one into the back seat which they covered with a blanket. Sam drove the truck to an abandoned warehouse and then went to work as usual.

Meanwhile Rock drove off, mingling with the morning traffic. He didn't realize he was speeding until a sheriff's car with sirens wailing, pulled him over. He didn't know what to do, but he had to stop. Two officers pulled up behind him and walked to the driver's side of the car and knocked on the window. Rock looked out at the man and said, "What's wrong officer?"

"You were driving erratically and thirty miles over the speed limit. Please get out, we are going to search your car." The other officer opened the trunk and called out, "Look at what I found here Robert, three duffle bags filled with money."

Rock slid over to the passenger's side, opened the door and tried to run away. It was all just a bad memory now.

CHAPTER

23

Rock was fit to be tied. He was entitled to his money from the robbery and now he'd left it in the closet at his old apartment. He was going back immediately to see if it was still there.

Rock drove to Beatrice's house and banged on the door. When she saw him she smiled. "It took you long enough to get here," she exclaimed. So she found it Rock thought.

"Undoubtedly you know why I'm here, you didn't spend it all did you?"

"No, but finders, keepers," she said.

"Bull-shit, Beatrice, you know it's mine and a good Christian woman like you knows what's the right thing to do."

"You're right, but I want something for babysitting it."

"Ok, how does fifty thousand sound?"

"You've got to be kidding! You must have five hundred thousand dollars in there, at least! How about sixty thousand?" she contested. After all Rock had paid his dues she thought. "Seventy-five thousand," she came back firmly and left to fetch the money.

When she returned, Beatrice thrust the bag in his arms, "The cash will help me get what I want."

"And what is that?" he asked.

"I shouldn't tell you but there's a very handsome man about seventy years old renting the place. I would like to keep him here permanently."

Rock couldn't help but laugh. No fool like an old fool, he thought amused. He hoped lover-boy didn't die on her but that was her problem.

He tapped her on the shoulder and wished her good luck then he was on his way.

Now he has his money back, but what would he do with it? He thought about putting it in a Cayman Island account but nixed that idea because it wouldn't be accessible to him. Then he remembered there was a bank on almost every corner and he'd wondered how they all survived. I'll help them out and put the money in a few of them under assumed names. He would have the monthly statements sent to Ellen's address until he moved on, but that was up in the air now too.

CHAPTER

24

Gus Cook was a well-known gumshoe but not for his business finesse. He used to be the best, but over the years the bottle got him. He was picked up regularly for DUI and after a new investigation firm moved into the area he was almost forgotten.

Gus and Sam Smith had been buddies and were often seen down at the Wild Turkey, passing the afternoons away, drinking themselves into oblivion.

When Gus heard about Sam's drowning, he cursed and punched his fist through a wall. He and Sam had gone fishing many times. Gus was a true man of the water, always putting safety first; everyone in the boat had to wear a life vest at all times. Sam also used to be a certified scuba instructor and knew the depths of these waters had claimed many lives. He never would have been so careless as to have fallen off his boat and drown. Gus was motivated by his friend's death so he sobered up and began investigating like he used to.

First, he got into his old Chevy and drove out to the river. The crime scene tape was gone, so he thought the police investigation was over and he was free to check things out for himself.

Gus took a metal detector and combed the area but came up with no clue. He examined the ground that had been trampled by many feet and found nothing. He scratched his head and wondered what to do next.

The boat was pulled up on the bank, so he walked over to it to see if he could find anything there. He noticed that one oar was intact, but the other one was slightly bowed, possibly from hitting something hard with it. Gus shrugged his shoulders. It could be a clue but that was a little far-fetched. The only other thing he saw was a crumpled pack of Marlboro cigarettes. He knew Sam smoked but he bought 505's because he wanted to save money by smoking a cheaper brand. He put the pack in his pocket but didn't think it was a clue. Disappointed, he left the scene.

Next, Gus visited Sam's watering hole. When the bartender saw him, he put a scotch and water on the bar for him to drink. Gus held up his hand, "Not today, Ollie. I'm working."

The bartender raised an eyebrow thinking it had been a long time since Gus turned down a drink or raised a finger to do anything constructive. Gus sat on a bar stool and put his elbows on the bar. "Sam played poker in the back room didn't he?" he asked.

"Sure did, every Wednesday night."

"Who played cards with him?" Gus asked although he knew.

Ollie answered, "Rick, Rock and Jason; and of course Sam, God rest his soul."

Gus nodded his head. For some reason, The Brinks truck robbery came to mind. Rock spent ten years in prison but the other men involved were never identified. Strange, he thought that the number of men was the same number as the guys that played cards. Maybe he was on to something but it would take more evidence than he had to get the authorities to open up the case. Gus wasn't going to give up. He figured his friend was murdered and he wanted to nail whoever did it.

Sam's funeral was put off until the autopsy results came back and then he was cremated. When his ashes were returned there would be a short ceremony at the grave site.

A month after Sam died, Rick called Rock; he was surprised to hear from him. Rock liked him because he was a hardworking man who cared about his job; unlike Sam who was not ambitious at all and was disliked by most people. Rock had no desire to talk to any of them.

When a shiny blue Volvo convertible approached, Rock didn't recognize the driver until he pulled up to the curb. "Get in," Rick shouted as if he had just seen Rock yesterday. He got in the car and looked at the suave man in the driver's seat; Rick looked like he just had a photo shoot for Esquire magazine.

Rock realized he didn't know what to say to the stranger sitting next to him. He groped for words and finally said loudly, "Long time no see. How yah been?"

Rick straightened his shoulders, "I'll have you know, you are looking at the new President of the Community Bank!"

"Congratulations," Rock rendered.

Rick acted like Rock hadn't spoken. "I'm now invited to the social events given by all the dignitaries in this county and I'm head of the Banker's Association."

Rock cut him off before he could go any further but couldn't resist asking, "Do you ever have any time for Tracy or your kids?"

Rick shrugged it off, "The kids don't care if I'm around or not, all they care about is their friends."

"And Tracy?"

Rick flung his arm out and had a look on his face of someone that was about to tell a lie. "She enjoys all the attention - thrives on it. I swear she looks ten years younger."

"How nice for you," Rock jeered.

Rick concentrated on navigating through a few cars that were parked on the small road that twisted around the cemetery. An equally small amount of people were gathered where a small hole had been dug to accommodate an urn. A short, unkempt woman clutched the vase to her chest. Next to her stood a boy and a girl about twelve years old, with clothes that were wrinkled and old looking. If anyone saw them on the street they would think they were orphans.

Rock looked at the meager crowd. A few of the people were probably neighbors, but two people stood out. One was a middle-aged man wearing a suit. He vaguely remembered seeing somewhere. Then there was the woman in a bright red dress, inappropriate for a funeral. "Who is that?" Rock asked, pointing at the woman.

"I don't know what she is doing here, but that's my wife!" he replied. "I'm going over to talk to her to find out just why she's here."

As Rock strode away, the woman turned around and he couldn't believe his eyes. From the backside the woman looked fantastic, but when she turned around she looked at least sixty years old. Her face was creased with wrinkles and her eyes had dark circles under them. That is Rick's wife? She didn't look happy or like Rick had described at all.

He saw Rick approach her then grab her arm and pull her away from the others. He could see they were arguing and turned away. Nothing was as Rick wanted him to believe it was. Rock couldn't believe how much Rick had changed.

Rock felt the urge to get rid of him but squelched it. The man was disillusioned and fooling himself into thinking he was living a beautiful life. I'm not that stupid Rock thought. Rick's life was built on quicksand that Rock was sure would engulf him at any time.

Rock listened to the short talk by the pastor and paid his respects to Sam's wife. After the short service, Rick joined him and they drove back to town. Neither of them spoke during the fifteen minute ride.

When Rock got out of the car, he said, "Thanks for the ride buddy, see you later." He watched Rick drive away and knew that it would never happen.

CHAPTER

25

Now all the men that had stolen the money were gone and Rock was still not satisfied because of his part in it. He got on his knees and asked God to forgive him, but felt he wasn't listening. The only thing left was to recapture Ellen's love that he wanted so desperately.

On the way back to Ellen's, Rock stopped at the floral shop and bought a dozen red roses. He imagined the surprised look she would have on her face when she saw them.

It wasn't quite five o'clock when he got there, but he realized she wouldn't be home from work yet. Rusty wiggled all over when Rock walked through the door. He scratched the dog behind the ears and together they walked into the kitchen. Rock badly needed a bottle of beer, so he took a Bud from the fridge. He and the dog went into the living room to watch a movie while they waited for Ellen to get home.

He drifted off to sleep and woke up with a start. It was dark outside so he knew it had to be late. He couldn't believe Ellen wasn't home yet. What if something was wrong? Rock started thinking of the horrible things that could have happened to her. He tried to calm down by thinking she must have had a late showing. She'd be home soon, he told himself.

Another hour went by and Ellen still was not there and he became more anxious. Rock considered calling the police but didn't want to have any contact with them. As far as they knew he wasn't in the area. And he knew his disguise was still working because even at the funeral no one knew who the stranger was.

Rock got off the sofa to let Rusty back in and watched him pick up his bowl, looking for his supper. It was then that he spotted a note taped to the refrigerator door. How could he have missed it before?

Rock removed the note and saw that it was written in Ellen's small, neat handwriting. It read: Rock, I've decided I need a break; my world is closing in on me. Marie can run the office for me while I am gone. I'm going to visit my Aunt Dorothy. Please take care of Rusty. E

Rock read the note over twice. Who was Aunt Dorothy anyway? Ellen never mentioned having an aunt. Nor did she say where she lived so Rock couldn't contact her there and she didn't say when she'd be back.

He looked at the dog and said sadly, "She's left us, Rusty." He seemed to know what Rock told him because he whined and walked over to Rock and placed his head on his knee.

CHAPTER

26

Gus kept thinking he had missed something down at the site of Sam's drowning, so he drove back there to check it out again. This time he would extend the search area to look for clues.

He fanned out from where the footsteps were found and couldn't find anything. Gus was ready to leave when he saw a large rock jutting up from the ground. He walked over to it and on close inspection saw that a hole about twelve by twelve inches had been dug into the ground and had the stone covering it with weeds growing around it so it wasn't easily seen. Could this mean anything? Gus wondered.

Then a thought came to him. It was the right size to hide a bag of money in; one of the four men that robbed the truck could have hid the money there. Gus thought about each man and tried to decide which one was the most likely to have hid it. Two of them were dead so that left Rick and Rock.

Rick was the most likely candidate because he'd purchased an expensive car recently. But then he was making big bucks now so he could afford it. Rock was the only man left, but no one has seen him. He was probably not even in the area. However, he would investigate the two men's bank accounts to see if anything looked unusual, such as having too much money, but that was too easy. Without any other leads he would be at a dead end. He would check them out tomorrow. He needed his liquor fix for the day so when he got back to his office he slammed several shots of bourbon and passed out resting his head on the desk.

When Rick went into his bank to make a deposit, the manager called him into the office. "Sit down," the man suggested, so Rick sat across from him. "You should know that someone has been here asking questions about your account. We also think your account has been hacked, so we assigned you another number. However, it is a temporary fix. This person is good and will soon find this number out too. I suggest you change your name on the account and lead him on a wild goose-chase.

Rick was incensed. "Who in God's name could be doing this?" The first one who came to mind was Rock, but why? He had money of his own. Suddenly a thought occurred to him. Now he remembered where he'd seen the strange man was at the funeral. It was that old drunk Gus that no one hired anymore. Why is he doing this?

Rick was quiet for so long, the banker was concerned. "Do you have an idea who it could be?" he asked.

"Possibly," Rick replied.

"I think you should call the police. This person could be dangerous."

Rick got up from his seat. No way would he talk to the police. He would handle this himself.

Rick fumed as he drove to the drunk's office. He had stopped home on the way. His kids were at school and his wife was probably out shopping. He was only there a short time, then hurried on his way.

When he got to Gus's office he knocked on the door, but no one answered, so he shoved the door open. There he was, passed out at his desk with an empty bottle of bourbon beside him.

Rick took the gun from his pocket and shot Gus in the back. His body jerked then fell to the floor.

Rick hurried outside and looked to the right and to the left. No one had seen him so he got into his car and drove away. He'd never killed a man before and he was surprised it gave him such a rush.

CHAPTER
27

A homeless man dug in all the dumpsters looking for food and clothes. He found something in each one and placed it in a mesh bag he carried with him. He'd have to hide it when he got back to where he stayed under the bridge. The others would steal it from him.

The bum's sack was almost full, but he'd look to see what he could find in one more dumpster. There wasn't anything of interest except an old pair of tennis shoes way down at the bottom. He jumped in, pushed away some of the bags of garbage and grabbed the shoes. To his surprise, the shoes were dirty but they looked like brand new. He quickly took off his old shoes that had holes in them and stuffed his feet into the new ones. They were a little too long but the width was good. He threw his old ones into the dumpster and walked to the bridge, pleased with the haul he'd made, but wished he'd found a beer too.

He was thirsty and needed some liquid. Now he'd have to take a drink from the public water fountain in the rest area. He took a long drink and sat down on a bench and watched a few of the other homeless from under the bridge walk by him. Their bags were half full and he could see they were envious of his full bag.

Maybe I should find another place to stay the bum thought. The word would get around and everyone would be looking for him to steal from his bag. He decided to stay at the soup kitchen that night. There was an ally behind it with a little storage shed; he'd be safe there for a while.

The cops patrolled the area to see that all was quiet. The only time there was a problem was when two of the street people fought over a bag with a bottle of wine in it. When that happened the culprits were thrown in jail overnight and then let out the next morning because there was nothing else to do with them.

After one of the fights, the guy with the full bag was involved in a scuffle. He was taken to jail and as usual he was frisked by the police. When Murphy saw his tennis shoes, he demanded to know where he got them. "In a dumpster," the man said defensively.

"Hey," detective Murphy called out. "I think I've found something here!"

Another officer came running and when he got there, he stared at the shoes. "Holy shit!" he exclaimed. "Are those what I think they are?"

"Yup, I think so; we'd better call the chief at once."

CHAPTER

28

Rock was lonesome for Ellen. It had been two months since she left and Marie kept calling him to see if she was back yet. She was frustrated because she hadn't heard from Ellen either and finally confessed to Rock that running the real estate office was too much for her and she needed a break.

Rock could sympathize with her. He wanted Ellen to come back too, to show her how much he loved her. How could he have been so selfish by thinking of only his own needs and acting like an animal when they had sex.

One evening Rock had just gotten home from work when he heard the front door slam. Rusty began barking furiously so he went to see who was there. He was shocked to see Ellen wrestling her suitcase in the door. Rusty launched himself at her, nearly knocking her to the floor. She dropped the bag and got on her knees and hugged him while he licked her face.

Rock cleared his throat loudly. "What am I, chopped liver?" he asked feeling left out.

In response, Ellen ran to Rock and hugged him fiercely, "God, I missed you!" she exclaimed.

"Not as much as I missed you," Rock returned.

She changed the subject. "I'm starved, have you got anything to eat around here?"

Rock put his arm around her and led her to the kitchen. "How about I fire up the grill and we have steaks?"

"That sounds wonderful! I'll run upstairs and take a shower."

"Can I come along?" he asked suggestively.

"Down boy, you can wait until later."

"Promises, promises," Rock laughed and went to get the charcoal and to start the grill. He would make sure their sex was perfect that night, he thought with a smile. Life is good again.

CHAPTER
29

A week later, the station got a frantic call from the office next to Gus's. "Please, come quick!" a man's voice cried. "We've had a putrid smell around here for a week. I think it's coming from the office next door. Hurry, everyone is dreading what you might find."

When the chief and an officer arrived, they had to break the lock to get in. The potent smell hit them in the face as they saw Gus's body. "Go back to your office!" the chief shouted to all the people that had gathered outside the door. "Open the window and turn on the fan," he ordered the officer with him. The body was blue and bloated so the chief knew he'd been dead for some time. He called for an ambulance and asked that the medical examiner be notified of the death. He knew he would be investigating this as a murder for sure.

The chief sighed. A lot of bad things were happening in his quiet, little town. He couldn't imagine what had happened here, but he vowed to find out. It was his job and he desperately needed to get to the bottom of it.

When the chief got back to the station he went to his office to think. He put his feet up on the desk and leaned back in his chair. He closed his eyes and thought about all that had happened lately. He didn't think it was a coincidence that there were four poker players and four robbers. He wondered if they were connected. At very least he would check into it.

CHAPTER
30

Besides the slow nickel and diming, Rock's old car was requiring more and more repair. The transmission was now starting to slip and the oil light was on constantly now. It would cost him an arm and a leg to fix it.

Rock pulled into the Ford dealer's lot because he noticed a non-descript gray sedan with a standard transmission and manual windows and it wouldn't raise any red flags if he drove it. On second thought, he was wearing a disguise, so no one will recognize him anyway.

Down the street there was a Chevrolet dealership so he decided to look around there. In the showroom there was a bright red sports car that he loved. After looking around a little more, he realized he didn't want a plain car after all. He kept going back to the sports car so he decided to buy it. To hell with everybody else Rock thought. He was a working man making good money; he could buy himself a new car if he wanted to. People bought new cars every day of the week.

After haggling over the price, the salesman then agreed with Rock's price. He signed the paperwork for the transfer of tag and title then the salesman asked him if he wanted to take out a loan for the balance less the trade-in. Rock shook his head no and told the man he would pay cash. The salesman thought, 'You sure can't judge a book by its cover.' Rock shook the salesman's hand and told him that he would be back the next morning bright and early to pay for and pick up the car.

Rock drove to the closest bank he had money in. He walked up to the window and asked to withdraw thirty thousand dollars from his account. It was a large sum of money so the teller had to call the bank manager to approve the transaction.

The manager was a serious looking man wearing a black suit and tie. Rock thought he looked like a mortician. After scanning over the paperwork, he initialed his approval. Suddenly Rock realized that he couldn't take that amount of cash to the dealership so he asked the teller to prepare a cashier's check for the amount. The manager nodded at Rock and walked away. He wondered if the man would remember the incident. It was a good thing the account was in a different name.

The next morning Rock waited while the salesman verified that the check was good. He was all smiles and shook Rock's hand as he handed him the keys to the car.

Rock felt like a little boy that had just stolen a handful of candy from the hidden jar. It was sure fun spending money he thought, having to remind himself that he couldn't spend too much of it, or he'd call attention to himself.

When Ellen saw the car, she had mixed emotions. It was awesome, but where did he get the money? So she asked him outright about it.

"Honey," He answered, "I've been saving some money from working and got a good trade-in; I got a really good deal."

Ellen looked at him suspiciously. "How will you pay for the rest?" she asked.

Rock laughed. "Not to worry my dear, I have a small loan that I can easily pay off."

Ellen must have bought his explanation as she asked him, "Can we take it for a spin? It's been a long time since I've ridden in a new car!"

"Sure. Let's go!"

CHAPTER

31

Rick nervously read the newspaper each day so he could keep up on any progress made on finding the unknown killer of old Gus the gumshoe. So far they didn't have a clue, but the chief hinted that they had a suspect.

Rick worried that he would be caught; that somehow the police would find out the gun used was his. He decided he had to get rid of it quickly. After much deliberation, he thought he would throw the gun in the river where it would sink and never be found.

He got into his fancy car and drove to a State park located along the river. He swam out to where it was about ten feet deep and dropped the gun. The water was clear and he could see it settle on the sandy river bottom where it sunk until only the barrel was visible. Relieved, he swam back to shore.

He was getting out of the water when someone called his name. Rick turned around and saw his neighbor and his family setting up a tent to camp-out. Rick waved, trying to look casual and headed for his car.

Joe ran toward him, "Wait up," he hollered.

"I have to go. I just came here for a quick dip," Rick answered.

"I have something to tell you," Joe insisted, "Wait up."

"Damn-it!" Rick said under his breath. He didn't want to be seen there and especially not by someone who knew him so well.

"I wanted to invite you to a block party on Saturday night. Do you and Tracey have plans?"

Rick couldn't think of any excuse why they couldn't go. What if Joe mentioned he saw him down here swimming? "Not that I can think of, but I'll have to check with my wife," Rick returned.

"Ok. Do that" Joe said. "Have Tracey call my wife."

Rick went back to his car distressed. Why the hell did something like this have to happen? He drove home with an old saying repeating itself over and over in his head, "Everything happens for a reason." He turned up the radio to try to drown it out but it didn't stop until he got home. Now Rick had something else to worry about, was he losing his mind?

Of course Tracey was delighted they were going to the party. "We'll finally get to meet the Robinsons." she exclaimed. The family had moved in, two doors down, three weeks ago and they hadn't talked to them yet. Tracey was glad because the new neighbor's boy looked the same age as their Johnny and they could play together.

Tracey hummed all Saturday morning while she baked a luscious chocolate cake to take to the party. Since it was a BYO, Rick intended to take a bottle of white wine for him and Tracey to share.

Everyone was already there when they arrived. Johnny's grandmother was late coming to babysit which put them a little behind schedule. When they walked in, Joe ran over to greet them. Rick's heart was nearly pumping out of his chest but he knew he had to put on a happy face, "Hi pal," he said. Then he screwed up, "Long time no see."

"You rascal!," Joe exclaimed, slapping him on the back, "I just saw you swimming down at the river a few days ago."

Rick wished he was anywhere but there. Tracey looked strangely at Rick, "What did he say?" she asked perplexed.

"Didn't you hear him?" Rick asked defensively. "He said his family went swimming down at the river."

Now Tracey knew he was lying, "No, he didn't," she cried. "I heard what he said! Explain yourself."

"I don't want to fight in front of our friends," he stated firmly and grabbed her arm. "We're going home and I'll drag you if you don't come willingly." All of the people watched as they walked away without saying a word.

To lighten the mood, Joe laughed and threw his hands up saying, "What did I say?" and he laughed harder. Inside he felt rotten. Why did he say what he did? Every man needs some time alone and he'd spoiled Rick's.

CHAPTER
32

The chief and Murphy called the homeless man Milo for lack of any other name. This particular man had stayed at the jail many nights so they knew him well. The three of them sat together in the interrogation room. A recorder sat on the table in front of them.

The chief could see that Milo was shaking because he was so nervous. "We won't hurt you Milo," the chief assured him. "We just want to ask you a few questions." The man didn't say anything, but nodded. Murphy moved to a chair away from him because the odor coming from his body was overpowering. "Those are very nice shoes you have on," the chief said. "They look brand new. Where did you get them?"

"Don't know."

"Come on, we know you work Hall Street."

Milo lowered his eyes and answered, "In a dumpster."

The chief asked, "Where was it located?"

"You said it, on Hall Street."

"Will you show us which one it is?"

Milo shrunk back, "I can't show up with any cops, no one there trusts you. I wouldn't last a day."

The chief nodded. "We'll do it in a way that you won't be in any danger," he promised.

Changing the subject, Murphy asked, "Did those shoes have mud on the soles of them when you found them?"

Milo shook his head yes. The chief stood up and ordered, "Take the shoes off Milo. They're evidence now."

Milo shook his head no. "I have no shoes to wear," he screamed.

"Settle down, we'll get you some." He didn't tell Mile but he knew that there were several pairs in the morgue that hadn't been disposed of yet. "I'll have Murphy get a pair for you." He pointed to Murphy and he left the room to get the shoes. Milo clutched the shoes tightly. The chief didn't say anything because he knew he didn't want to give them up until he had another pair to replace them.

Murphy was back within minutes holding a pair of black and red tennis shoes just like the other ones. "They're size ten and a half so I think they will fit."

Murphy saw Milo's eyes light up when he saw the shoes and he held out his hands to take them. He bent over and tried them on, grinning from ear to ear, so apparently they fit.

The chief thanked Milo for his cooperation and the three of them started for the door when the chief stopped and said, "You two go up front and wait for me. I'll get there as quickly as I can," and hurried away.

A short while later they met up in the lobby. The chief held out a brown paper bag which he gave to Milo. The man opened it and sniffed. Inside there was two ham sandwiches from the machine and a container of coffee. Milo excitedly took out one of the sandwiches and devoured it instantly. Murphy and the chief waited for him to finish the other one and led him to the door. The chief felt good about it; who knew when the poor guy had eaten last?

CHAPTER

33

Burt Collins lived upstairs above Collins' Dive Shop. His father started the business in 1956 and since his death his son had built the business up to be the most highly regarded in the field. Burt now offered diving classes that were always filled to capacity. People from all over the US came there to learn to dive. There were fifty people enrolled in the current class.

Of course with that many clients, Burt had to hire more certified instructors. The program was only offered to people between the ages of eighteen and thirty because persons of that age had quick enough reflexes to survive in the water.

The course itself took three months to complete. It was a rigorous training schedule of diving three hours, three times a week. Many people failed or dropped out for a variety of reasons so the actual completion rate hovered around fifty percent.

Because Burt was now forty-five years old, after his classes were finished, he would hang up his tanks and enjoy life like others did.

At exactly nine o'clock am, his ten students met him on the dock. They all boarded a flat, wooden raft-like vessel propelled by a huge one thousand horse motor. On the end of the raft was a supply room with medical supplies, several tanks filled with oxygen, life jackets and diving equipment.

Burt started the motor and trolled along the river's edge for a while, then came to a stop about two hundred yards from shore. The students with tanks strapped on their backs were ready for their last fifteen minute dive and jumped into the water one by one. When the life lines attached to the rig were taut, Bert knew the divers were as far away from the boat as they could go. He watched the clear water carefully to be sure no one was in danger.

In only five minutes a young diver came up to the surface and shoved his goggles up on his head. He tugged on the rope attached to the raft and Burt pulled him in. He could tell the man was agitated so he asked him, "Are you sick Ray or are you freaked out at something you saw down there?"

In response, Ray pulled a Colt 45 out of the mesh bag he carried and tossed it on the deck.

"What the hell," was all Burt could manage as he gingerly picked up the gun with one gloved finger, snapped open the chamber, spun the wheel and saw that one bullet was missing. He snapped it shut wondering why a weapon like this had been found in the water.

When everyone was back on board he quickly motored back to shore. After he had given everyone their certificate and said good-bye to them all, he got in his car and drove to the police station. Burt located the chief, walked up to him and said, "Hello chief, I've got something for you to look at," and placed the gun in his hand.

The chief stared at it and asked, "Where the hell did you get this?"

"One of my divers found it in the river about twenty-five feet down. I looked it over and it appears one bullet is missing."

The chief turned the gun over checking for serial numbers and there they were. He looked at Burt and said, "You just earned a thousand dollar reward."

"What for?" Burt asked perplexed. Was the chief putting him on?

"I do believe you just found the gun that murdered a man." He left Burt standing there while he took the gun to the lab to be processed.

The chief was enthused to have found what he thought was the murder weapon in one case, but was also dismayed. He had both the tennis shoes with prints that fit the ones found at the river and now the gun that likely shot Gus, but he wasn't close to solving either case. What should he do next?

CHAPTER

34

When the morning "Chronicle" reported the gun that shot the old investigator had been found, Rick lost it. I have to think. I know they can trace the gun to me because of the serial number. I'm a dead duck, he told himself, panicking. I'll have to find a way to frame Rock again he thought. It would be the only way he could avoid going to jail for the rest of his life. But he needed Tracey to help him do it and she wasn't speaking to him. I'll get out of this somehow, he thought, I'm a pillar in this community; I'm the manager of the bank, the head of the Better Business Bureau and a city commissioner. It shouldn't be hard to frame Rock, we did it before. After all he was a con now. This time he would be put away for life.

CHAPTER

35

Rock felt amiss that he hadn't been noticed at Jason's funeral. His casket had been closed because of the extensive injuries. All of the team members and the grieving family were there. Since he hid behind the outskirts of the crowd, he hadn't had the chance to offer his condolences to Jason's wife Ann. Although he was very angry at the man the last time they'd met, he felt he had to do the right thing.

It was a Monday and it was slow at Richard's Plumbing and some of the workers were going home early. Rock drove slowly by Jason's house and saw Ann was outside pruning the flowers. He thought it would be a good time to talk to her so he pulled the car up to the curb and got out. Ann looked up and saw him but apparently didn't recognize him and kept working with her flowers.

"Hi Ann," Rock called, walking toward her. She peered at him, then got up and hurried toward the house. "Wait!" Rock yelled. The woman stopped but didn't turn around. Rock caught up with her and said, "Ann, I want to talk to you."

"Why?" she asked emotionlessly.

"I want to offer my condolences."

"It's a little late, isn't it? You weren't at the funeral or the lunch afterward." Then she began to cry and reconsidered, "Oh, you may as well come in. The sun is hot and I was going in anyway."

The two of them entered the house that had plastic covers over the furniture. The wall between the kitchen and the living room was torn down leaving a pile of debris on the floor.

"Remodeling?" Rock asked.

"Yes, I'm doing a complete renovation of the house. I've always wanted to do it but Jason didn't agree with me. Now that he's gone I am going through with it." Ann's eyes filled with tears and she looked like she was about to cry again. "We'll have to sit in the kitchen; it's the only place the contractor hasn't torn apart yet."

They sat at the kitchen table and looked at each other. Ann broke the silence by saying, "You are disguised and it took a while to recognize you."

Rock nodded in agreement. For the first time he really looked at the woman. Even in the state she was in, she was pretty. She had red curly hair that framed her face and huge green eyes with an olive complexion.

Ann saw Rock looking at her and smiled for once. He's looking me over she thought and it feels good to feel attractive. "I heard you got out of jail but I haven't seen you around."

"That's because I don't want to be seen."

Ann nodded, "I can see that. What do you want?"

"Even though Jason and I had our differences I feel for you and your family. How are you doing?"

Ann grimaced, "Wonderfully well. Jason left me well fixed. He had an insurance plan for five hundred thousand dollars that I didn't know he had. When I went to see the insurance agent he told me Jason had purchased it about ten years ago."

That explains where some of his share of the money went Rock thought. Clever! No one would have thought of that. "So, you're Ok then, I wanted to be sure," Rock explained.

Ann brightened, "I'm getting the house fixed up like I want it; I'm also seeing someone, and the kids like him too," she said happily.

Rock was surprised but knew she should move on. "How have the kids adjusted after Jason's death?"

"Remarkably well. Although it was rough at first, now they talk about him once in a while, but time heals."

Rock got up to leave because he knew their conversation was over and she obviously didn't need his help. "I'll be leaving now," he told her.

"Come and see me anytime," she told him but he could see in her eyes that she didn't mean it.

Rock took her hand and squeezed it, "Maybe I will," he said, but knew he never would. "Say Hi to the kids for me."

Rock left with a good feeling about Ann. She obviously had everything under control and he was happy for her.

CHAPTER

36

Rick was frustrated because Tracey avoided him completely. She was too embarrassed by the fiasco at the party to talk to the neighbors. Nor would she attend any business functions with him. Of course sex was out of the question.

If he could only go back in time and change things he would; he wouldn't have married Tracey at all. She was several years older but Rick had ignored that because she ran with the elite circle and came from a wealthy family. He had figured that her wealth would help him climb the ladder of success.

Rick dreamed of entering into politics, probably becoming Governor of the state, then elected to the senate and who knows, eventually it was possible he could become president. None of these dreams could come true unless he was back on good terms with Tracey. If he could accomplish all this, no one would ever connect him with the Brink's robbery.

Tracey was always complaining that their house was too small for the family. Rick thought that if he bought her a new, extravagant home that she would forget all about her disappointments with him. Yes! He thought that would be the best idea he could come up with and opened the phone and looked up the number of Solar Realty.

Ellen herself answered, "Good afternoon, Solar Realty," she said.

"Hey Ellen, how are you?" Rick asked.

"Fine, who's calling?"

"It's Rick, you know the manager of your bank?"

Ellen knew of him of course. "Hello Rick, what can I do for you?"

"Tracy thinks we need a larger house so I wondered if you had some listings that would fit the bill."

Ellen hesitated because she knew Rock was at odds with him but business was business. "What is your price range?"

Rick thought about it but told himself that he was rich and said, "I can buy anything I want."

Ellen was shocked but answered, "I have several. When can we get together?"

"Is one o'clock tomorrow afternoon Ok?"

Ellen looked at her calendar. "I have another showing at eleven o'clock but I'm sure I will be finished by then."

"Good, good I look forward to seeing you."

"Tomorrow then," Ellen said and hung up the phone. She was still amazed that he'd chosen her company. She couldn't wait to tell Rock about it.

The next afternoon Rick walked into the real estate office and put his hand out for her to shake, with a huge smile on his face. When Ellen shook it, it felt cold and clammy. She quickly pulled her hand away. "Let's get right down to business," she said walking swiftly to her desk.

Rick sat across the desk and looked at her expectantly. Ellen held up some pictures of houses that she had in a file folder and handed them to Rick. "Here are photos of homes I thought you might be interested in."

He took them from her and scrutinized each one, but quickly handed them back and said, "These look like cookie-cutters to me," he said obviously disinterested.

"They are beautiful homes in nice neighborhoods. I have others to show you but they are over your budget."

"Don't pay attention to what I said. Show me the best and most expensive ones you have, the sky's the limit!" Rick exclaimed.

Ellen put the pieces together immediately. Rick was one of the three men who had stolen the money and let Rock take the rap for them. So that is the reason the two men were at odds. Well, that sheds another light on things she thought.

Ellen looked through her files and came up with three more pictures to show Rick, all with the price tag of more than a million dollars. He looked them over and his face turned red, "These are too expensive. I was thinking of paying half a million at the most."

Ellen couldn't resist cutting him down, "I thought you said the sky's the limit."

Rick cleared his throat, "I didn't think you'd take it literally."

Ellen didn't answer but handed him three more pictures. Rick looked them over and said, "I guess they'll do," he replied reluctantly.

Ellen stood up, "Thanks, Rick," she said putting on a fake smile. "Come by tomorrow at nine in the morning." She walked him to the door and watched him get into his new Volvo. I wonder how much money those guys got, she mused, and who his other partners were.

Ellen drove Rick to an affluent subdivision on the edge of town. She stopped the SUV in front of a sprawling brick home which was painted white, had black shutters and colorful flowers peeking out from the window boxes. "This is the first house you saw, let's go see the inside."

Rick didn't move. "I don't like it!" he remarked.

"Really? Why not? What would you think if I told you it's only five hundred ninety-five thousand dollars?"

Rick's eyes brightened but he repeated, "I said I didn't like it! Let's go see the others," he said angrily.

Ellen looked at him sharply. "Rick what's the matter with you?" she asked him staring straight in his eyes.

"If you must know the police chief lives in this subdivision and he isn't one of my favorite people, and his kids would go to the same school as mine."

Ellen started the SUV again and drove off sure Rick wouldn't like anything she showed him. She stopped at another house built in the Tudor style. The outside was white stucco with dark finished wood accents. The front door was very heavy, dark wood with a bird carved into it. To Ellen's surprise, Rick said "I like this one, let's go in and see it!"

The house had three bedrooms and two and a half bathrooms, one a Jack and Jill for the kids and a large master one lavishly appointed with a huge shower, double sinks and a soaker tub. The master bedroom was very large with the light filtering through the windows. Rick frowned when he saw how small the other two rooms were. When he and Ellen walked into a galley kitchen his dislike was evident. "Tracey wouldn't like this at all! It's too small and doesn't have an island. She likes a gas stove and this is electric and the granite counter tops are too dark. Let's get out of here now before I get sick!"

Ellen was so disgusted with him she wanted to kick him out of the car and leave him standing there by himself. But she told herself to settle down. She only had one more house to go and she'd be through. She thought it was an act of futility because he would never buy a house, but she would follow through. Ellen wondered why she'd squandered away the morning with Rick when she could have been doing something productive.

Next she took Rick to an older home on the edge of town. In this area there were large, two-story colonial homes. All the yards had manicured mature lawns with stately old trees. Ellen stopped in the front of the house and looked fearfully at Rick. To her surprise he said, "That's just what I'm looking for!"

She decided to cut him down to size. "It's a lovely home but it's out of your price range. It's listed for eight hundred thousand dollars."

Rick's face fell, but then he smiled, "Can you talk them down?" he asked.

"Possibly ten thousand dollars, not anymore."

"I don't even have to see the inside, I want to buy it!" As an afterthought, he unenthusiastically said, "I know Tracey will love it!" Actually it was the opposite of what she would like. She loved large lots preferably several miles out of town.

"I'll sign the papers and bring the money in to you tomorrow. By the way, if you can't get the owner down a few thousand don't worry, I'll take it anyway."

"I assume you will get your mortgage through your bank."

Rick shook his head, "No Ma'am, I'll pay cash," he said firmly. At the same time he wondered if he should have bought the place. He calculated how much money he would have left and cursed silently at his foolishness. He would only have peanuts left.

Ellen was flabbergasted when Rick came into sign the papers and brought a duffle bag full of money with him. She watched wide-eyed as he shook the big bag and a multitude of banded hundred dollar bills spilled out onto her desk. "Where did you get so much money?" she asked him, but she knew.

She considered calling the chief but discarded the idea. She'd let Rock handle it she thought, but she was afraid of what he'd do.

CHAPTER

37

The chief decided to concentrate on Gus's murder investigation instead of Sam's death for the time being. He sent Murphy to Gus's office to look through his files. It wasn't long before he hit pay dirt; there was a folder with Sam's name on it. The scribbled notes showed that Gus knew who was responsible for Sam's death.

Murphy was elated and knew the chief would be too. The old man was a mainstay of the area, how could he be involved in Sam's death? If he was found guilty he would go to jail and they'd throw away the key. Murphy hurried back to the station with the evidence.

Marie had taken a few days of sick leave and didn't know what had transpired while she was gone. When Ellen showed her the money and told her what had happened, she couldn't believe it. "What do we do now?" she asked, "I never heard of something like this before. Are you going to tell the chief about this?

"Not yet. I will wait and see what he finds out about Gus's death."

In the meantime Tracey was surprised that Rick had purchased her a new home. It never occurred to her to ask him where he got the money. Instead, she told him all the remodeling she wanted to do. Rick didn't know how to tell her there wasn't any money to do it.

Ellen and Rock sat down to have a glass of wine to relax before they had dinner. "Honey," she said excitedly, I had another lucrative sale yesterday."

"You're on a roll," Rock said smiling.

"Wait until you hear what it was!" Ellen exclaimed.

"I'm listening."

"Your old buddy Rick bought a lovely old home for beaux-coup money."

"What?" Rock asked. What is wrong with him? He's spending money like a drunken sailor. Someone was bound to notice. On the other hand, Rock was glad that he would hang himself. The chief would put two and two together and figure out that he was one of three men that he was looking for. Rock pretended he wasn't interested. "Bully for him," he declared and finished his wine. "I'm hungry, why don't we have dinner and then dessert?" Rock wiggled his eyebrows at her.

"I thought you'd never ask," Ellen said smiling.

CHAPTER

38

"I love you for buying this house for me," Tracey cried launching herself at Rick, hugging him fiercely around the neck. "When can we start remodeling? You know I want to paint the walls and get new cabinets for the kitchen." She wrinkled her nose. "The kitchen is so outdated."

"We'll begin those projects soon," Rick hedged, knowing he couldn't put her off much longer. He was sick of her harping at him about it, so he came home early, less and less, not wanting to hear her nag.

Rick frequently dropped into the real estate office to chat with Ellen. When she wasn't in he flirted with Marie and took her to lunch often. Then she started meeting him for drinks after work. She was clearly enamored with him, and they ended up going to bed together. Things got heavy so soon that they started meeting at a motel on the outskirts of town regularly.

The couple who owned the motel knew who Rick was and they were disgusted with him for what he was doing. "I'm going to tell Tracey about this!" Mrs. Withers told her husband.

"Mind your own business," he retorted firmly. "Just let it be."

Marie was missing work a couple of days a week and Ellen was worried about her. Her eyes had dark dark circles under them and her skin was as white as a ghost. "Come into my office," Ellen said to Marie. Sullenly the girl followed Ellen in and sat down. Marie had lost weight, as if she hadn't eaten for a week. Ellen looked at her with concern.

"What's the matter with you?" she asked kindly, "You've missed so much work lately, are you sick?"

Marie shook her head. "My Mom has been feeling sickly, poor thing. I've been taking care of her," she lied.

"I'm sorry but you are getting behind with your work and soon I'll have to get someone to help you out. Could I pay for a nurse to tend to your mother? This is obviously running you down."

Marie began to cry. Ellen got up from her chair and put her arms around the girl. Then Marie cried out, "I'm pregnant and I don't know what to do!"

At first Ellen was angry at her but then she felt sorry for the stupid girl. Hadn't young people heard of birth control? There was no excuse for getting pregnant anymore. "Who's the father?" Ellen demanded.

Marie cried even harder. "I know he loves me."

"If he does, get married."

"He's already married," Marie replied defensively, "But he says he doesn't love his wife and he's going to get a divorce," and she began sobbing.

Ellen was appalled by her words. "What a louse!" she exclaimed. "You fell for that old line? He'll never leave his wife. He's played you for a fool!"

"He loves me!" Marie insisted.

"Sure he does," Ellen returned sharply. "What are you going to do, get an abortion?"

"No," Marie cried, "He wants me to, but I want to keep the baby."

"Number one, you can't afford it, and number two, who's going to babysit while you work?"

"I don't know."

"There you are. There is no way you can take care of an infant. Get old lover boy to pay for the abortion and send him on his way."

Marie hung her head. "He says he doesn't have any money because he made a large investment lately and there isn't any left."

Ellen thought about what Marie had said and it became clear who she was talking about. "That horses ass," she said under her breath. How can I help this nit-wit? Just wait until Rock hears about this.

When Ellen told Rock the story, he lost his temper. Rick was never like that before. He shook his head resolutely. Money is surely the root of all evil he thought. I won't have to kill him now, Rock told himself. He knew Rick would hang his own self. Rock realized when things got bad enough Rick wouldn't be able to face the music. The man is a coward. I don't have to lift a finger. He will take his own life eventually.

CHAPTER

39

The chief looked over the results of the tests taken in Gus's office. He cursed. "God damn-it," there weren't any clues there. Only Gus's fingerprints were found on the liquor bottle and the glass that stood next to it. The residue on the door knob had smudged finger prints that were Gus's and one partial, which was only partly visible. It could have belonged to anyone.

The chief realized that the murderer was clever enough to wear gloves; in fact in his haste he had dropped one on the floor. It was an expensive faux leather glove in a size that would fit nine tenths of the men who wore them. The chief would check to see if any store in the area sold them, but if this guy was shrewd enough the effort would be futile. More than likely they were ordered from the many catalogues he received in the mail.

Murphy was sent to Gus's office to go through his things. He didn't find anything of interest except a daily planner. On the day that Gus was murdered there was a hand written notation of a meeting at twelve o' clock noon but it didn't say who with. Frustrated, Murphy threw the planner across the room. It landed against the wall with a thud.

When Murphy picked it up, he noticed a six by nine picture hanging on the wall. It was of Gus with his arm around Sam. They wore waders and Sam held a fishing pole in his left hand. Well, could this be a clue? Gus was a friend of Sam's. Sam had died several weeks ago, so he couldn't have murdered Gus for revenge. He would take the picture and show it to the chief, thinking nothing would become of it.

Murphy finished his job and took Gus's meager belongings to the station. He put the box on the chief's desk. The chief looked through it but didn't find anything of interest. However he took a long look at the picture. So Gus knew Sam. So what? They looked like buddies in the picture.

The chief rolled up the yellow crime scene tape and put it back in the box. It was then that he realized he hadn't connected Sam with the men that played poker every Wednesday night in the room behind Tink's bar. That's a dead end too, he thought because Sam had drowned, and Jason had been killed in a car crash.

That left Rock who was out of prison, but no one knew where he was. The law had checked with old Mrs. Simmons but all she knew was that he had a lot of money. Where did he get it? The chief would like to know, but because his men hadn't seen Rick in the area, he couldn't interrogate him.

The only other man left was the well-known mucky-muck Rick. Because of his fine standing in the community he didn't want to touch him with a ten foot pole. The chief sighed. It was a long shot, but it had to be done. The chief wanted to pass this job off onto Murphy, but he would have to talk to Rick himself.

When the chief pulled in to the driveway of Rick's house he was struck with the opulence of it. The home was in an exclusive area and looked perfectly groomed on the outside. It had fresh paint and the copper roof shone like it was new. Obviously the house cost a pretty penny, but in Rick's position at the Community Bank he must have made a lot of money.

The chief reluctantly knocked on the door. A frazzled Tracey answered it. When she saw the chief, she was shocked and wondered why he was there. The chief noticed the deep wrinkles on her cheeks and the pock marks that covered her face. They stood out and made her look even more unattractive than she was.

Finally Tracey recovered from the jolt of seeing the chief standing on her door step. "Why chief," she said putting a smile on her face. "Do come in," she invited. He took off his visor cap and followed her into the house. "Please sit down," she said and led him to a large, overstuffed chair.

The chief looked around the room. All the furniture looked expensive and new. He wondered if the bank paid so much money that Rick could afford all this. I'll have to check that out, he thought, also his bank account. Maybe that would reveal something that was out of line.

"May I give you something to drink? Coffee, Tea, a soft drink?" Tracey asked sweetly.

"No, thanks; I'm not here on a social visit. I have to ask you a few questions."

Tracey wasn't surprised. What had Rick done? she wondered. Well, she'd find out soon enough.

The chief cleared his throat then began his questioning. "Did Rick know the investigator that was murdered?" the chief asked.

Tracey shook her head no. "He felt he was superior to him."

The chief expected that answer. "Did he know Sam Smith?"

"Yes, of course, he played poker with him every week," she answered.

"Does Rick have a lot of money like he never had before?"

"Yes. But he got a raise at the bank and I didn't think anything of it."

"Enough to buy this house and a new sports car?"

Tracey answered defensively, "I was surprised about the car because our old one was only a year old. But I'd been hounding him for a bigger house, so that didn't surprise me."

"I see." The chief thought for a minute then asked, "Has Rick done anything unusual lately?"

Tracey was taken aback by the question so she paused before she answered. "I've called the bank for him in the afternoons but more often than not, he's not there."

"Really? Any idea where he'd be?"

"No, I don't," Tracey replied obviously distressed.

The chief knew he'd hit a sore spot. It was time to stop questioning her. He got up from his chair and prepared to leave. He turned to Tracey. "I'm sorry to ask you questions about your personal life but I promise the information you gave me will be safe. You have my word. I won't tell anyone."

"Thank -you," Tracey answered, "I believe you chief."

The chief digested what he had just heard. Rick's money was of interest. He wondered where he got it and it seemed like he was overspending lately. The chief didn't think his personal life had anything to do with the case, but will check it out anyway. For now, he would have to put this investigation on the back burner because he had other cases to take care of.

CHAPTER

40

Marie dragged herself into Solar Realty where Ellen was waiting for her. "Sit down!" she insisted. Marie sat down afraid of what Ellen would say.

Ellen wasted no time. "Marie, you look like hell. Your hair is greasy and your eyes have bags under them. In short, you are no longer an asset to my company. I will have to put you on leave until you come to your senses and end your affair with this married man."

Marie began to cry. "I can't. I'm having his baby!"

"I will help you if you will show me you can forget him and move on."

"I can't do that, I love him!" Marie shouted.

Ellen took five hundred dollars out of her purse and shoved it across the desk to her. "Take this. It will pay for an abortion."

Marie shook her head no. "I want his baby!" she cried.

"Don't be stupid, if you do he'll drop you like a hot potato."

"No he won't!"

Oh yes he will. I'm sure he already has children of his own. Believe me, he doesn't want to have a bastard to support."

Marie cried harder. "He won't answer my phone calls anymore and I haven't seen him for two weeks."

"Can't you see what's happening? He's dropped you, no matter what he says."

Marie looked wide-eyed at Ellen. "That's not true!" she screamed.

Ellen lost it. "Who is this jerk?" Suddenly she knew who it was. "I've figured out who it is. Believe me I know his wife."

Ellen shoved the money closer to Marie. "If you don't take the money and get an abortion, I will call her and tell her the whole story."

"You wouldn't," Marie cried.

Ellen made a move to pick up the phone. Marie jumped out of her chair and ran toward the door. "You're lying! You wouldn't betray me!"

Ellen retorted, "Oh yes I will young lady, just watch me!" she hollered back, slamming her palm on the desk. When Marie ran out the door, Ellen felt terrible because Marie was like a daughter to her.

To hell with it she thought. I'm going to make the call anyway. She hoped Rick would be charged with having sex with a minor, in addition to robbing a Brink's truck, and that he would be put away and they'd throw away the key. She also made up her mind that she'd tell the chief too. Ellen was sure he'd be very interested in this new wrinkle that had come up; Rick had paid her cash for the new house he'd just purchased.

The call to Tracy would have to wait until later.

CHAPTER

41

The chief's visit had rankled in Tracy's mind and she couldn't stop thinking about it. It had opened her eyes and when she analyzed her life with Rick suddenly the facts seemed very clear to her. It was shortly after their disagreement at the block party that he started to turn over a new leaf. They went out to dinner whenever she suggested it and he took her anywhere she wanted to go, even shopping which he hated with a passion. She should have known something was wrong when he bought the beautiful home for her when she had begged him to for years. Tracy knew that he was feeling guilty for something but although she racked her brain she couldn't imagine what. Rick was always in a good mood, like he should be, she thought. He was living the life he craved, rubbing shoulders with the affluent men in town and holding offices in many organizations. Rick was admired and looked up to by the people in town because of his presidency of the Community bank. The only thing that bothered Tracy was the fact that he spent money like water. She was sure he didn't make that much money at his job. Rick also had some investments, but he hadn't made good decisions about them, so they weren't producing like they should.

Tracy wanted to know why. So she planned to ask someone who would find answers, I could hire an investigator. But she didn't have any money of her own. Rick always kept his money, making her ask for some every time she needed it. Tracy had come from wealth and wasn't used to doing this, so she decided to ask her folks for the money, which she hated to do.

The phone rang four times at the Carlson's mansion in Tampa. Tracy was about to hang up when her mother breathlessly answered the phone.

"How are you Mom?" Tracy asked. "You sound out of breath."

"I was sitting on the veranda enjoying a Tom Collins," she laughed. "It's so hot here today."

Tracy got right to it. "I need some money," she said flatly.

"Whatever for? Remember, you get your trust money in six months. Can't you wait until then?"

Tracy thought quickly. "I decided to get a face lift. If I want to hang on to Rick, I'd better look as good as I can."

Her mother huffed. "Why won't Rick give you the money? He had enough money to buy himself a new car, didn't he?"

"Please Mom," Tracy begged.

"Oh alright. I'll send you ten thousand dollars by Western Union. It should be there in a couple of hours."

Tracy jerked her arm up in the air. When she received the money she could find what Rick was up to. If she couldn't she would die trying. An hour later the phone rang and when Tracy answered, she was surprised to hear her father's voice. "Hi Dad!" she greeted him.

His voice came back in a no nonsense tone. "What is this about Sybil sending you ten grand? The story that you're getting a face lift is bunk. Rick makes good money."

Tracy didn't know what to say, but finally answered flatly. "I think he's having an affair."

"That Son-of-a-bitch, I never thought he was for you anyway."

"Dad...."

"Forget the ten thousand, I'll send you five because you'll have to pay an investigator."

"I don't know any."

Horace thought for a minute, "I'll tell you what, I've used one by the name of Barnes. The police department uses him. Let me see if he's available and I'll get back to you."

"Thanks Dad," Tracy replied sincerely.

"Later," he replied and hung up.

Good old Dad to the rescue Tracy said to herself. He was always there when she needed him.

CHAPTER

42

Ellen had a fierce headache when she got home from work. She went directly into the kitchen cupboard and took out the aspirin. Rock looked at her with a worried expression. "You've been working too hard lately and you're probably run down. I hope you're not getting sick."

Ellen shook her head no. "No," she countered. "It's just stress."

Rock took her by the hand and led her to the living room. "Sit!" he ordered.

"I don't know how to begin but things are complicated. First of all Marie won't be working for me anymore."

"Why not? If that's the case hire a temp until she returns."

"It's not that simple. She's pregnant and insists on keeping the baby."

"Who's the father?" Rock demanded.

"If I tell you, you'll probably hurt him."

"Who?" Rock cried angrily.

"Rick," Ellen answered without emotion, but she looked like she was about to cry when she said it.

Rock jumped out of his chair. "Asshole!," he cried "How do you know this?"

"I just put the pieces of the puzzle together. She told me he was married and had children. He told Marie he loved her and was going to leave his wife. It's the same old story."

"And?" Rock prodded her.

"She said the man was well fixed and I immediately thought of Rick suddenly dumping a fortune on my desk for buying a house. Then Marie told me he couldn't afford to pay for an abortion because he'd just made a large investment."

Rock rubbed his chin, thinking. "The man has completely changed, maybe that's the reason. One thing for sure, we have to do something about it. I'll take care of him," Rock promised.

"No you won't. You said that before and haven't done anything yet!"

"I'll take care of him immediately!"

"How?" Ellen asked, afraid of the answer. "I'm going to tell the chief and that's final."

Rock looked at Ellen and shivered. "Please don't do that Ellen," Rock pleaded. He was sure the stolen money would come into play and Rick would squeal on him. Someone should stop him before he opened a can of worms. For the first time Rock was sorry Sam and Jason were dead.

The next day Ellen called the police station and asked for the chief. She was told he was out on scene of a serious accident on Highway 24. "When will he be back?" she asked.

"I expect him soon."

Without giving it a thought, Ellen blurted "Tell him I'll see him in half an hour," she told the dispatcher.

"Who is this?" he asked.

Ellen hung up the phone without answering. She grabbed her purse, put the closed sign in the window and drove to the station.

Ellen sat in the lobby of the station, anxiously awaiting the chief's arrival. The deputies kept staring at her wondering what she could possibly want from the chief.

"Hey Lady," the chief greeted Ellen. "Come on into my office." She followed the chief and waited until he closed the door behind them. When they were seated, she quickly told him the full story. The chief looked surprised at first, but then decided he wasn't all that surprised. I've finally got the break I need, he told himself with satisfaction. "Thanks Ellen," he said sincerely.

"Will you let me know how this all comes out?"

"I'm sure it will make the headline in the Chronicle," he replied. He never cared for Rick anyway. He was a slimy bastard as far as the chief was concerned.

CHAPTER

43

Rick was certain he was being followed. The same blue Chevrolet was behind him everywhere he went. Why would someone be following him he asked himself?

Rick took a left turn, then a right, trying to lose the car behind him. Then his opportunity came. He raced through a yellow light and the other car was held up by the red light. Rick stomped on the accelerator and shot down the road. Before the car could catch up, he quickly turned into an alley and waited. When he saw the car go by, he made a U-turn, and joined the traffic going the other way. He hit the steering wheel and laughed out loud.

Rick was doing a little surveillance himself. He kept tabs on Marie wherever she went. Unfortunately she was always accompanied by Ellen or her mother. He hadn't called her for weeks and she hadn't tried to contact him.

He had watched the girl go into the local library and she was alone! He waited until she came out with her arms full of books, heading into the parking garage to her car. She stumbled and dropped a book.

Rick was out of the car in a flash. When Marie bent over to pick up the book, he was on her. He shoved her hard in the middle of her back and she pitched forward landing on the concrete, books flying. Marie clutched her stomach and screamed when he kicked her in the abdomen. She tried to cover herself, but he kicked her again.

Rick looked around anxiously; no one saw him crouched behind a car because they all were hurrying to go home after work. Marie had passed out. He looked at her and saw blood staining her clothes; some of it trickling down to the cement beneath her. "I hope the little bastard died," he raged under his breath.

He realized he had to get out of there quick, before anyone saw him. It was busy in the parking garage so he dashed to the upper level where his car was parked. In minutes he was gone and out into the traffic. She won't be able to identify me, he thought confidently, I hit her from the rear and after that she was too busy trying to protect herself. He was sure she didn't see who he was.

Rick only had driven a few blocks when a Ford sedan rear-ended him, catapulting his car into the one ahead of him. The crash caused Rick's head to hit the windshield, the glass shattered and blood streamed down his face. He was unconscious until he awoke on the stretcher in the back of an ambulance on his way to the hospital.

"What? Where's my car?" he yelled.

The EMT patted his shoulder, "Settle down. We're taking you to the hospital for treatment on your head. It's full of glass fragments and you probably have a concussion."

"I don't understand," Rick mumbled.

"You were in a serious car accident. You are lucky to be alive my friend."

Rick tried to sit up, but he was restrained by the IV connected to his arm. "Where is my car?" he shouted.

"It has been towed to a salvage yard. The car is demolished and can't be repaired. I'm sure you will be hearing from your insurance company."

"What? It's only four months old!" Rick shouted.

"That's all I know, let the insurance company take care of it. I'm sorry man."

"Great!" Rick said to himself, he not only lost his beautiful new wheels, but now he was placed in the close proximity of his attack on Marie. He worried that the police would find out he was near the scene where she was beaten. What excuse did he have for being in that neighborhood at that time?

"Lean back and relax, we're almost at the hospital," the medic said.

"Call my wife; tell her where I am," he cried. For the first time in his life he was afraid. No one else was close enough to call. Suddenly he felt terribly alone. Rick wasn't even sure if his wife would respond.

The next morning the headlines in the paper read, "Local Leader in Car Crash." Under the headline was a picture of Rick's demolished car.

Every morning the chief sat at his desk with a cup of coffee and the morning news before he began to work. When he opened the paper and saw the headlines he felt like swearing a blue streak. Now he wouldn't be able to question ole Ricky boy for a while. "Damn-it to hell," he swore aloud as he opened his desk drawer to pull out his bottle of Jim Beam. He poured a healthy shot into his coffee. He knew it was too early in the day to drink but he kept the bourbon there, for days like this. If this isn't the shit, I don't know what is, he thought, as he gulped the liquid down. Instantly he began to feel better as the warmth crept through his body. The chief pinned on his badge, put his hat on his head and was ready for the day.

The first thing on the agenda was to check with the Sheriff's office to get the particulars on Rick's accident. For some reason, he had a premonition that things were going to get ugly soon. The chief took a deep breath, bracing himself for anything that came up. He'd handle it. After all, he was the chief of police wasn't he?

CHAPTER

44

Tracy got the mail in as she did every day. She leafed through the pile and cast aside several magazines and requests for donations. Among them was a bill from Master card. She usually just gave it to Rick, but this time she was curious enough to open the envelope. She stared at the charges and lost it. There were purchases from four different restaurants and many other charges from Berg's Motel. Tracy wondered where she'd heard that name before but then remembered she had driven by it the other day. What on earth was Rick doing there?

But suddenly she knew he was taking some other woman there. That was why he wasn't at the bank when she called in the afternoon. She'd been too naive. Things had been going so well between them she hadn't suspected anything was wrong, even when she found a smear of red on his shirt. She had just cleaned it off and threw the shirt into the washer. It was clear to her now that it was lipstick.

Tracy paced the room entertaining the idea of taking the kids and going down to see her mother and father for a while, but they were in school. There was no way she would pull them out for several weeks or more and have them miss that many classes.

She ran to the phone to call the investigator. She had paid him a thousand dollars down payment but to date she hadn't heard from him. Mr. Osborne answered on the first ring, "Action Investigators, Ozzie speaking."

"Hello, this is Tracy Rayburn. I haven't heard from you and I wondered if you have some news."

"I was just making out a report for you," he answered.

"Did you find anything out about Rick's habits?"

"Of course I did. Your husband is a cheater, you were right to suspect him. Look, I think I should give you this information in person."

Tracy didn't want to hear the truth so she cut him off. "That won't be necessary, you've found out what I wanted to know. Thank you very much for your time," she said and hung up. As soon as she did, she knew she shouldn't have. For God's sake, she didn't even know who the woman was.

Tracy went into a full-blown rage, she wanted to hurt Rick or better yet cut off his dick. "No more sex for you buddy," Tracy said bitterly. The phone rang loudly and she tried to ignore it until the constant ringing got to her. "Hello!" she screamed into the phone.

A calm voice asked, "Am I speaking to Mrs. Rayburn?"

Tracy tried to pull herself together and replied in her normal voice, "Yes you are."

"This is the Chaplain from St. Paul's Hospital. Your husband has been in an automobile accident and I'm calling to notify you as his next of kin."

Tracy forgot everything she'd said about him earlier and panicked, "Is he dead?" she cried.

"No Ma'am, he isn't. We won't know the extent of his injuries until we're finished running the tests."

"I'll be right down!" she exclaimed.

Tracy was driving faster than she should. When she realized she'd left in a rush without any money, she pulled in the next seven eleven and tried to use her debit card to get some cash. She tapped in two hundred dollars and waited for the cash to come out.

Instead a sign flashed, "Non-sufficient funds." Maybe I'm asking for too much she thought. So Tracy asked for one hundred dollars this time with the same result. She kicked the machine in anger and ran back to her car. She'd drive to her bank to see what was wrong. When she was almost there she remembered it was past seven o'clock and the bank was closed. She tried not to think about it, but in her heart she knew that Rick had drained their bank account too and began to cry. What did

I do to deserve this? She turned the car around and drove back home. She couldn't bring herself to see Rick that night or maybe ever again.

The next day Tracy went down to the court house and applied for a restraining order. She could imagine Rick's surprise when he couldn't get in his own house! The next thing she did was go to the police station to see the chief. When Tracy walked into his office, he really wasn't surprised to see her. He noticed how rough she looked, her hair looked like it hadn't been combed, and her eyes were red and swollen.

"Please sit down Tracy," the chief said kindly and helped her into a chair. Then he sat down and turned on the intercom, "Have Murphy bring me a cup of coffee, and an aspirin if anyone has one. Tracy, what have you come to tell me?" he asked her.

CHAPTER
45

It had been two weeks that Marie hadn't either shown up or called Solar Realty. Ellen desperately needed someone to man the office when she was out, she didn't have a choice. She'd have to hire someone else so she placed an ad in the Chronical. After getting no results, she called the professor of real estate sales at the local university, who was a friend of hers.

"I can think of one girl that completed the class last semester. As far as I know she hasn't found a job yet. If you'd like, I can call her to see if she wants to meet with you. I'll give you a call back to tell you how I made out."

"Great!" Ellen enthused. "Tell the young lady I pay well and am very interested in talking to her," Ellen replied.

"By the way, her name is Anita Long. I think you'll like her."

A week later the professor hadn't called Ellen back. She was very disappointed and run down from working too many hours doing two jobs. She developed a terrible cold and when it spread into her chest the doctor told her it was walking pneumonia, Rock put his foot down.

"Ellen," he said firmly, "You have to close the office and stay home. Rest is what you need and I insist you do it. If not I'll leave on vacation."

"You'll what? Leave me in the lurch when I feel like this?"

Rock decided he had to get tough. "Yes," he declared without really meaning it. "I'll give you a choice. It's either your job or me, make your choice."

Ellen began to cry. "If you put it like that there's no contest. I would choose you every time and you know that.

Rock was relieved. "Alright then Ellen, I'll go down to the pharmacy and pick up the prescription the doctor wrote you. By the time I get back I'll expect you to be in bed." Rock angrily left the house.

Ellen went straight to the bedroom because she knew Rock was right. Why couldn't she ever take anyone's advice? This time he was right. Ellen called Rusty to come with her and the dog followed her to the bedroom. When he jumped up and lay down beside her, Ellen ruffled his hair. "You're my buddy," she crooned and the dog sighed deeply. In five minutes both of them were sound asleep.

Later that night Marie's mother called. Without saying hello she began speaking. "This is Lillian Banks. I'm worried because I haven't seen or heard from Marie for a week, I'm sick with worry. I've called the realty office many times and no one answers. Please, can I talk to Ellen to see if she knows anything?"

"I'm sorry, Ellen is ill and can't speak to you," Rock told her. "The reason you can't get ahold of her is because the agency has been closed. Marie hasn't gone into work because she's been too sick and she hasn't had anyone to run the office for her. Ellen tried to do both jobs but became ill over it. Have you called the police?"

"No, I haven't. I was sure she would come home." Her voice broke and Rock's heart went out to her.

"Do it at once!" he urged, "They will find her. That's what they do, it's their job."

"Alright," she conceded, "I'll do it right now." Lillian hung up without saying another word.

Rock decided to not tell Ellen anything about this. She would want to go look for Marie, sick or not.

CHAPTER

46

Murphy walked into the chief's office with his hat in his hand. He knew what he had to tell the chief would probably get him fired, but it was important.

"Hello chief," Murphy muttered.

"What's wrong with you? Speak up," the chief said sharply. "Get on with it. The phones have been ringing every five minutes. I swear the full moon is bringing out all the crazies."

"Chief, I….." Murphy said looking at the floor.

"Spit it out," the chief ordered. "What?" he asked loudly.

Murphy's words came out in a rush. "You know that hit and run on Main Street?"

"Yep, so what?"

"It was me that rear-ended Mr. Rayburn's car."

The chief was out of his chair in a second. "How in the hell did you do that?"

"I was following him in the unmarked and he stopped in front of me. I got the hell out of there before your men got there."

"I don't blame you, but where is the car? Is it completely wrecked? Judging by the damage done to Rick's, I'm sure it's a mess."

"Well, Sir it's down at Mel's Body Shop. The front of the car is, ah, rather smashed."

"Rather?"

"Back to where the seats were; I was lucky not to get both legs broken."

The chief looked him over. "You look Ok to me."

"Somehow I got out of the car by myself."

"I thought you said you drove away."

"To tell the truth the car only ran for a block. I left it in the middle of the road and took off."

The chief slammed his fist on the desk. "We'll have to ask the mayor to buy us a new car. You know he's always harping about not having any money, now this. You can bet he won't be happy."

Murphy hung his head.

The chief pointed a finger at him angrily. "If we weren't so short of help, I'd fire you. Instead, I'm putting you on desk duty for a month. You'd better behave or I warn you I'll make it longer. Now get out of here!"

Murphy slunk out the back door. For a few minutes he thought about quitting but he liked his job and needed the money. It didn't pay as much as it should, but he'd been a cop for twenty years and it was in his blood.

The chief picked up the ringing phone. "This is the chief," he growled. "This better not be bad news."

"It is. You'd better get over to Drake Street. We've found a half dead woman lying in the alley next to the library!"

"Jesus Christ," the chief swore. What else can happen? "I'm on my way," he said into the phone as he grabbed his hat and was out the door.

CHAPTER

47

Tracy's fingers trembled as she punched in the chief's private number. She hated to bother him, but she had a bad premonition and had to talk to him. She'd seen the article in the paper reporting the story of the pregnant girl that was found in the alley near the library, and was afraid Rick was involved.

"Chief here," he answered. Any call that came in on his private line was always bad news as only a few people had it. When he recognized Tracy's voice he knew that he was right, it was bad news.

"Chief," she said, obviously distressed, "I think the woman found in the alley was Rick's girlfriend."

This is worse than I thought, the chief moaned. "Why do you think so?"

"It's only a premonition, but I know I'm right."

"Tell me more," the chief said, immediately on the defensive.

"The investigator I hired reported Rick was seeing someone. He followed him and reported that he spent a lot of time with her. He even gave me a description and since then I've seen a girl that looked just like that at Ellen's office."

"That's a long shot," the chief replied shortly. "There are a lot of women who look like that."

"I know he went to the real estate office a lot. At first I thought it was Ellen he was involved with, but now I know better. Ellen wouldn't look at anyone else; she's too much into Rock."

"Ok Tracy, I'll look into it. You might be right. Stop thinking, will you?"

Tracy changed the subject, "Have you gone to the hospital to talk to Rick yet?"

"I've been too busy and the doctor wouldn't let anyone speak to him until now." The chief wondered why Tracy didn't know that. "Haven't you been to the hospital to see him?"

"No, haven't," Tracy answered coldly. "I don't care if I ever see the SOB again!"

The chief didn't know what to say to that so he simply said, "Take it easy. I'll call you when I know something."

After he hung up, he thought about all she'd said. He would talk to Ellen to see if she knew anything and if the girl had any friends, he'd speak to them too.

The chief badly needed Murphy's help, as he was the best. He'd like to rescind the order he'd given to transfer him to desk duty, but he couldn't because he didn't want to set a precedent.

CHAPTER

48

Rock never worked on weekends but Ellen did. Often clients wanted to see houses on Saturday because it was their day off and others only had Sunday's free.

Rock had already re-plumbed the cottage and gotten rid of the of the old cast iron pipes, replacing them with PVC ones. After that he painted the exterior of the cottage from white to a pale yellow color.

Rock had to tie up Rusty after he'd gotten inquisitive one day and decided to play with the paint can lid, that had some paint still on its underside. "Naughty dog!" he'd admonished him. The animal looked up with his big brown eyes. Rock honestly thought Rusty looked like he was going to cry as he slid on his stomach over to him and nudged him with his nose. Rock couldn't resist him, so he bent down and ruffled his hair.

"Alright boy, now you've got to get cleaned up," he said. The dog slowly followed him into the house as if he knew something terrible was going to happen. Rock went to the garage and got a bucket of soap and water and told Rusty to sit. He saturated a rag and attempted to clean off his nose and the longer hair covering his chest. Rusty wiggled and sneezed but Rock managed to remove most of the paint. However, when Rock really looked at him there was still a lot of yellow paint on his chest. "Your Mom is going to laugh at you if she's sees you like this. You look like a clown!" Rock laughed. The dog slunk away confused by the tone of Rock's voice.

Rock put his hands on his hips in despair and wondered what he should do. Finally he decided he'd have to cut his hair to get the paint completely off. He went into Ellen's sewing room and got a large scissors. Rusty saw him coming and tried to run, but Rock cut him off and told him to sit down. Rusty obediently did as he was told and waited eagerly for the treat he always got. "Not this time doggy," Rock said and began trimming his chest with the scissors. Rusty laid his ears back, but other than that he didn't move. Rock trimmed a little hair off, then a little more. Without realizing what he was doing, Rock had cut the dog's hair down to the skin. He looked at what he'd done with horror. "Oh my God," he cried.

Rock dashed into the bathroom and came back with some Vaseline. He spread it all over the dog's chest and hoped he would be alright. Actually Rusty looked terrible, about as bad as Rock felt. Ellen would kill him! Feeling guilty, Rock got a large milk bone out of the jar in the kitchen and offered it to the dog. He happily chomped it down and wagged his tail. Rock suspected Rusty realized his ordeal was over and he was back in Rock's good graces.

For some reason, the episode reminded Rock of Jason's dog. He remembered how much he'd loved his dog and wondered what happened to it. Rock decided since he had nothing better to do, he would try to find out. He got into his car and drove by Jason's house.

The back yard was still fenced but no dog was in sight. Rock pulled into the driveway, walked to the front steps and up to the door. He knocked and rang the doorbell, but no one came. Rock looked around and saw no car by the garage or in the circular drive so he concluded no one was home.

He was on the first step when the door opened. A maid in a gray uniform asked, "May I help you?"

Rock turned around to talk to the woman.

"Who are you?" she said gruffly.

"A friend of Jason's."

The woman peered at him through her thick glasses. "How did you know him?"

"We played poker together for years."

The woman sniffed. "You were one of those!" she exclaimed looking down her nose. Then she asked again, "What do you want?"

"Actually I came here to find out what happened to Jason's dog."

"That mongrel? The mistress gave him away to a couple after Jason died."

"Is he alright there?"

"Who's asking?"

Rock was irritated with all the questions so he asked her sarcastically, "What is this, twenty questions? I'm a friend of Jason's, do you understand that? I want to find out if his dog is alright."

If looks could kill, Rock would be dead. She spit out the words, "I guess he is alright and the couple that owns him is too. Jason left thousands of dollars to the dog and his keepers with instructions that he would be taken care of for the rest of his life. Those people fell into it. They go to Costa Rica once a year and that miserable beast stays at a doggie spa while they're gone."

"All Jason left Bonnie was this house and a mountain of debt. Obviously he thought more of his dog than he did his wife." She shrugged, "I just wonder where he got all that money," she said sarcastically.

Jason left all his money to his dog! Rock wished he could tell Ellen, but knew he couldn't. For the hundredth time he wondered what he should do with his. He laughed uproariously again. Rock took one hand off the steering wheel and stuck his thumb up. "I have to hand it to you assholes, at least you did something good with your ill-begotten money," he said out loud. Then he turned on the radio and sang along to the music all the way home.

When he got there he shaved and washed his hair six times to get the black color out of it. Now Ellen would have a fit over two things he thought and laughed loudly again.

However, when Ellen returned from work she didn't even comment about his his appearance. Neither did she ask where Rusty was when Rusty didn't greet her at the door. Instead she threw her jacket on a chair and sat down. "We've got to talk," she said in a no-nonsense voice. It sounded like a direction to Rock, so he sat down with a thud, waiting to hear what she had to say.

"Tracy came to see me today," she began.

"Really? What for?"

"To find out everything she could about Marie. She thinks Rick is the father of Marie's baby and is responsible for her beating."

"Good God!" Rick cried, "He turned out to be a criminal! The question is who will stop him?" Rock counted angrily.

"The chief came right after she left and asked about Marie too. I got the idea that Marie's case was a top priority. He emphasized he was on his way to the hospital to interview both of them."

Rock shook his head. "I know a lot of guys that have cheated on their wives but it never ended like this."

"Even though you spent ten years in prison, I don't think you'd ever do a thing like that!" Ellen finally noticed he'd gotten rid of his disguise and he looked like the Rock she had known before. "Why?" she asked staring at him.

"It's time for me to face the people in this town. Some of them have recognized me anyway and others seem to have forgotten what happened."

"I'm so glad! I wondered when you would come to that conclusion."

Rock got up from his chair and walked over to her. "Get up," he ordered.

Puzzled, Ellen got up. Rock threw his arms around her and gave her a bear hug.

"What is this all about?" Ellen asked laughing.

"I want you to be my wife," he said nonchalantly.

"Are you kidding?"

"Do I have to get down on my hands and knees?"

"No, I mean yes! You don't have to get down on your hands and knees, and yes I will marry you!" Ellen exclaimed. Then she looked solemnly at Rock. "I thought you'd never ask," she said smiling at him.

CHAPTER

49

The chief walked into Rick's hospital room. He was sitting in bed reading a book. He looked up when the chief came in. "I expected you'd show up sooner or later," he said.

"I'm sure you know that my deputy has been following your movements for a long time."

"I knew someone was," Rock replied defensively.

"We also know you were messing around with Ellen's young assistant."

Rick couldn't meet the chief's eyes and he turned his head away from him.

"You realize we have you dead to rights. My man followed you to the motel and talked to the woman who owns it. She told him you were a regular there and that you came with a girl once a week. My deputy showed her a picture of Marie and she admitted that she was the one with you. What do you have to say about that?"

"So what? A lot of men I know got a little on the side."

"Maybe they are smarter than you and don't get caught or they cover their asses better."

"Who ratted me out?"

"Your own wife; she's a smart woman. You should have known you couldn't fool her for long." Rick finally looked guilty. "Furthermore I'd like to ask you what you were doing on Drew Street at two o'clock Thursday. You should have been at the bank which is about ten miles away." Rick stared at the chief but refused to answer. "Funny how you were in the same area, at the same time Marie was assaulted." Rick's face flushed, but he still didn't say a word. "I'd lawyer-up if I were you," the chief warned. "I think you're going to need one." He stood up to leave then turned back, "Your bank account shows that you deposited thousands of dollars in it and in six months you have spent it all. What do you have to say about that?"

"I inherited a load of money from my uncle."

"Sure you did," the chief said sarcastically. "We can check that out too you know."

"Go ahead," Rick said defensively, but the chief could tell he was bluffing.

Marie lay inert on the hospital bed. Her neck was encased in a large, white collar that kept her head from moving. Her leg was extended on a frame above the bed. Her face and arms were bruised and her stomach was bandaged.

When she saw the chief enter the room she tried to cover herself with one hand. "That's Ok Marie," he said soothingly, "I'm a married man you know."

"Why are you here?" she asked, "I know this isn't a social visit."

"Of course not, I came to ask you a few questions."

Marie made a face but decided she'd better cooperate. "Go ahead," she said.

"I understand some married man impregnated you."

"He loves me! I wanted to keep his baby," Marie wailed then stroked her flat stomach. "Now I lost the baby because of the beating. Who would do something like that?" she cried.

"Calm down!" the chief ordered. "Think about it Marie, there's only one person who would want the baby dead."

"No, no," she cried. "He told me he was getting a divorce from his wife."

The chief had heard this sad story before. He tried to get her to tell the truth. "Who is this guy?" he asked hopefully.

Marie didn't fall for it and clamped her mouth shut.

The chief decided he might just as well leave. Marie was enamored with the jerk. He hoped she would come to her senses and incriminate Rick later.

CHAPTER

50

Tracy was unloading the dishwasher when she got to the silverware and fingered a large butcher knife. I should kill that cheating creep she thought. She placed it on the countertop and stared at it. The idea of killing Rick grew in her mind. Why shouldn't she? He'd betrayed his wife and family and deserved to pay for it.

Without thinking any further, she went into her bedroom and put on a pair of black jeans and a black hoodie. Then she placed a red wig on her head and put one of Rick's visor caps over it.

Tracy shoved the knife in the back of her jeans and was ready to go. She hurried out to her car and drove to the hospital. When Tracy got there only a few cars were in the parking lot. She looked at her watch and saw that visiting hours were almost over. She ran to the emergency door ad opened it, but the alarm went off so she opened the nearest door and quickly entered it. She found herself in the cleaning supply room. Tracy sat down on an overturned pail and waited. Someone would surely check out who opened the emergency door.

She waited for fifteen minutes then entered a hall that passed patient's rooms. A lone nurse was walking into one room and then another holding a tray. She was obviously giving out the nightly medication.

Tracy darted behind a cleaning cart and crouched down. The nurse walked by oblivious to her. When the woman was gone, she was on the move again. The Chaplin had informed her that Rick was in room 106 so when Tracy found it, she slipped into the room.

Rick was sound asleep with his back turned to her. She jerked the knife out from the back of her jeans and grasped the handle. Tracy crept to the bed, lifted her arm and plunged the knife in Rick's back again and again. He cried out as blood spattered out of the wounds.

She quickly wiped the knife on the bed's sheets then hurried from the room. A nurse was a few rooms down, so Tracy straightened up and walked slowly back down the hall. No one stopped her because they thought she was a late visitor leaving a patients room.

She drove home, had a stiff drink of Brandy and went to bed. Tracy didn't feel one ounce of remorse and was sleeping like a baby in minutes.

When the chief got the call from the hospital, he cussed and ran out the door. The world has gone crazy, he thought. It seemed everyone wanted to bump someone off.

CHAPTER
51

Rock got home early and followed the tantalizing smell coming from the kitchen. He saw that Ellen had made a chocolate cake for dessert and it was perfect for what he wanted to do. First he fingered back the frosting on one corner of the cake. Then he got a small box out of his pocket and removed an engagement ring. The two carat diamond winked back at him as he inserted it into the cake. Using a teaspoon, he smoothed the frosting back in place. Rock was satisfied and sat down in his chair to wait for Ellen.

Ellen arrived late and sat down looking beat. "Let's have take-out Chinese tonight," she suggested.

Knowing fortune cookies would be included, he tried to look disinterested. "I don't feel like Chinese tonight, why don't you just go down to Tillies' Diner and get a meatloaf dinner? With the cake you made for dessert it would be a great meal."

"I can't believe you'd turn down Chinese, it's your favorite. Are you sick?"

"No, but the boss bought lunch for all of us because it was his birthday. It was Chinese," Rock lied.

"Ok, I'm not very hungry anyway."

"Panicking Rock replied, "We at least have to have a piece of that good looking cake you made."

"Maybe," she said and Rock relaxed a little. After dinner, Rock rubbed his belly.

"I left room for a piece of that luscious cake," he declared.

Ellen wrinkled her nose. "I think I'll pass," she said.

"Oh come on, you can cut a little piece off the corner. Surely you have enough room for that."

"Oh, Ok, if you say so." Ellen looked at Rock puzzled that he would encourage her to eat some cake. Usually he would kid her that she would get fat if she ate too many sweets.

She sat down at the table and cut a generous piece of cake for Rock and a small corner piece of cake for her. He watched anxiously as she took a bite, chewed, and swallowed it. What the hell he thought, had she cut off the wrong corner? The next bite Ellen took, she stopped chewing and with a strange look on her face spit out the ring. It rolled across the table and stopped when it hit Rock's plate.

He broke out into laughter at Ellen's expression. He took his napkin and wiped most of the cake crumbs off of it and handed it to Ellen unceremoniously. Then he roared again with laughter.

When he looked at Ellen, she was staring at the ring with a serious expression. "It's beautiful, is it mine?" she asked.

Rock pretended to look around, "I don't see anyone else here," he said.

Ellen smiled and got up to wash the ring under the faucet. After she was satisfied it was clean, she buffed it off with a towel and slipped it on her finger. She held her hand out in front of her and suddenly realized the large size of the stone. She turned to Rock and asked bluntly, "Where did you get the money for such a grand ring?"

Rock didn't know what to say but came up with a lame answer. "I robbed a bank!" Woops, he chastised himself, wrong thing to say. Then he pretended to laugh it off. "Honestly, I've been saving something out of every paycheck."

Ellen wanted to believe him so she went over to him, sat on his lap and gave him a long and emotional kiss. "When are we getting married?" she asked with excitement.

Rock hadn't thought of that, "How about tomorrow?"

"That's too soon, how about next week?" she replied seriously.

CHAPTER

52

The chief talked to all of the employees from the eight o'clock pm until one in the morning shift. Since it was quiet during that time, they operated with a skeleton crew. All of the doctors had their rounds done and had gone home for the night. He talked to the head nurse and all the others.

Only one that worked the late shift on the first floor had seen anything. She told the chief she saw a man of small stature, walking down the hall shortly after visiting hours ended but didn't think anything of it because visitors often stayed a few minutes after closing time.

The security man had told the chief that the alarm for the emergency door had gone off, but when he checked it out, nothing was amiss and no one was found in the area. The alarm had gone off again later but he hadn't bothered to investigate because it malfunctioned all the time.

But the unknown man that was seen in the hall rankled in his brain. Who was it? It could have been anyone. The world was filled with men of that description. To be sure he would make Murphy guard Rick's door as part of his punishment until Rick was released.

Marie was definitely disillusioned so he ordered some psychological sessions for her.

Ellen had agreed to take her back after her treatments were over. Anita wasn't working out but she would keep her on until Marie returned.

C H A P T E R

53

Tracy was bummed out that Rick wasn't dead. The newspaper reported that the knife had cut through the muscles in Rick's back, but hadn't hit any vital organs. He was a lucky man.

Tracy began dropping in to see Ellen at noon and often the two of them went to lunch. She asked a lot of questions about Marie and finally Ellen got tired of it. After that, every time Tracy suggested lunch, she pretended she had appointments or a client was coming in. Eventually Tracy must have gotten the message because she stopped coming in or calling.

Tracy realized that Ellen had figured out that she was pumping her. She hadn't gotten much information, but what she knew made her hate Rick even more. She vowed to kill him one way or another before he could come home and she would have to take care of him. Tracy imagined many scenarios in which to kill Rick but all of them were flawed. With disgust, she gave up. She decided she would sleep on it and maybe an idea would come to her in the morning. She did have a brilliant idea. She suspected a candy striper served the patient's breakfast on Saturday mornings as it was a particularly busy morning for the nurses. She decided to call the hospital and find out what she could.

When a volunteer answered the hospital's phone, Tracy asked to be connected to the first floor nurses station. Mrs. Richards, a nurse answered. Tracy rushed on talking as if she was in a hurry. "I'd like to find out the name of a candy striper that works on your floor on

Saturdays. This girl was excellent. My mother was in the hospital in a room 201 and wants to do something for the girl."

"How nice of her, what is your mother's name?"

Tracy thought fast. "Mrs. Smith," she answered choosing a common name.

"I don't recall anyone by that name."

"Maybe you wouldn't, it was several months ago."

"I see, only a few girls are still working here since then. I think it must be Marilyn Hughes. She is an excellent worker. Marilyn plans to become a nurse one day."

"Do you know when she will work again so I can talk to her?"

"Saturday she'll be here at six o'clock on the dot."

"Thanks so much, I'll tell my mother. She will be delighted." Both of them said good-bye and they disconnected. Tracy wanted to jump for joy now that she had a fool-proof plan.

Three candy stripers arrived for work early Saturday morning. Tracy asked one of them if if she was working the first floor the Saturday before. "No, Sue was," the girl said pointing at a plain girl in a well-worn jacket.

"Sue!" Tracy hollered, "Could I talk to you for a minute?"

The girl jogged over to her. "Hi," she said cheerfully, "Can I help you?"

Tracy watched the other two girls to make sure they were far enough away. Tracy took a chance. "I have a feeling you could use a little extra cash, am I right?"

Sue blushed, and subconsciously brushed at her worn jacket. "Yes," she said quietly. Tracy pulled a fifty dollar bill out of her coat and handed it to the girl. Her eyes widened. "Is that for me?"

"Yes, it is, if you help me out."

The girl looked at her warily. "What do I have to do?"

Tracy reached into her pocket again and held a paper packet in her hand. "I want you to put this powder into the coffee of the gentleman in room 106.

"Will it hurt him?" she cried, suddenly afraid.

"Of course not; the man is my cousin and he likes sugar in his coffee. The doctor won't give it to him because he had type-two diabetes."

"I don't think so," she said and she turned away.

"Wait! Don't leave! Put this in his coffee and make his day." Tracy held out another fifty dollar bill and Sue snatched it from her hand. "Does this mean you'll do it then?"

"Yeah, yes," the girl answered nervously.

"Ok here it is. Don't let anyone see you do it, understand?"

The girl ran away and entered the hospital so she would get to work on time.

When Sue took the tray for room 106, she quickly dumped the contents of the packet into the coffee. She stirred the coffee until the powder disappeared. After she'd done it, she was shaking so badly that she walked into room 105. She quickly placed the tray on the table next to the bed and fled the room.

Suddenly she felt nauseated and put her hand up to her mouth, afraid she was going to get sick. Sue ran up to the desk and mumbled, "Mrs. Jakes, I'm sick, I have to go home."

The nurse looked at the girl's pale face and assured her. "Go home dear, we can handle things here."

Before Sue got off the floor, a code blue was announced over the loud speaker. The man was convulsing in his bed. A nurse pulled back the bed covers to give him a shot, but the man stopped shaking and lay still. His open eyes stared at the ceiling. There was no doubt that he was dead. Sue didn't know she had killed a man nor did it make the news because he was an unknown figure and wouldn't make interesting reading.

Tracy only found out about the wrongful death because her housekeeper's sister was a nurse at the hospital. When she heard, she collapsed at a restaurant and was taken by ambulance to St Paul's Hospital. Now Rick, Marie and Tracy were all there. Everyone that knew the whole story couldn't believe it.

Of course the chief was always briefed by the medical examiner, so he knew of the man's death. But when he heard Tracy had collapsed and was rushed to the hospital, he smelled a rat. He picked up the phone and demanded that there was to be an autopsy on the man that had died at the hospital. Could it be possible that whatever killed the man in room 105 was meant for Rick in room 106? He was going to find out if it was the last thing he did.

CHAPTER

54

When Rock was alone he had a lot of time to himself. He went over all things that had happened after the robbery and was convinced Jason took his own life. Obviously the pressure of getting rid of his money was weighing on him. Jason had convinced himself he was better off dead than alive if he was going to be caught and end up in prison.

Rock was always puzzled why Jason had called him the day before the crash and apologized for his part in sending him to prison. Why then, not earlier, or not going with the plan at all. Rock was going to seek the truth and find out for sure if Jason committed suicide.

Rock contacted the chief and asked him to have his men check Jason's car over again to see if they had missed something before. The chief had told Rock that investigation was over and done, the case was closed. Rock persisted and finally the chief succumbed to shut him up.

Several days later the chief called Rock and apologized. He said he was wrong, that he should have conducted the search himself. He found out that the brakes had been tampered with and if Jason had been driving fast, he couldn't have stopped. He speculated that a deer might have run in front of the car or he could have swerved to avoid a collision. The chief begged Rock to keep the development to himself because divulging the new evidence wouldn't change the outcome.

Rock knew he was protecting his ass, but didn't want to go through the ordeal of proving that Jason's car was tampered with. It would wreck the chief's career and he was a good man, always working diligently at his job. Didn't everyone make mistakes? God knows, Rock thought, that he'd made enough of them. In the end Rock kept his mouth shut and the chief was grateful.

Rock thought more about the situation the robbery had caused. Families had been torn apart and everyone's life had changed and not for the good. As far as he could see there was no way to fix it. Rock reflected that the pay back he'd planned and the circumstances that followed had taken care of his planned revenge. Rock was sure God's intervention had a part in it and thanked him for what he'd done.

Now Rick was the only one left alive. What plans, does he have for me, Rock wondered.

CHAPTER

55

After a month in the hospital, Marie's wounds had healed and her doctor declared she could go home. Her love for Rick had turned to hate and she too thought of ways to pay him back for what he'd done to her. Something told her she should look at his past so she called Ellen to look on her computer to see if she could find something out.

At first Ellen refused, but then she reconsidered. She loved Marie like her daughter and she decided she would help the girl anyway she could. After a week, she had dug up the sorted details of Rick's past.

When he was twelve he was caught torturing the neighbor's cat and spent two years in juvenile detention. Because he was a juvenile, it was like a slap on the wrist and he was released to his mother. A year later his mother died and Rick went back to his devious ways. His next offense was bullying a classmate of his. He punched her out and put her in the hospital. He still wasn't eighteen so he spent more time in detention. When he was older, he dated a girl for over a year and his family thought he was straightened out. Rick was getting married and everyone close to him was relieved. Before long the girl went missing, but when the girl's family contacted the authorities the case was dropped for lack of evidence.

After that he moved to Grand Junction and became a success. Rick was intelligent and moved up the ladder quickly. No one looked into his past so after some time he was promoted to president of the Community Bank and was a pillar of the community. He seemed to live an exemplary life until the robbery. No one even considered Rick as a suspect because of his stature in the community.

Ellen reported Rick's past to Marie but there wasn't any record after he moved to Grand Junction. The information that Ellen presented, infuriated Marie even more and she planned how to stage Rick's death.

When she got home, Marie could think of nothing else but to imagine many different scenarios to kill him, but none of them seemed right. After a while she thought the plan she devised would work. She didn't waste any time putting it into action. By that time Rick was well and had resumed his duties at the bank. Marie began calling him every day, begging Rick to see her and rekindle their relationship.

At first he ignored her, wondering why she could possibly want him back, but being the person that he was, he began seeing her again. Marie pretended she was still in love with him, but when he wanted to have sex with her she always had an excuse. Either she had cramps or her period or she was too tired.

One night he suggested they park at lover's lane, located in a State Park on a rocky bluff. Rick was ecstatic because he thought she would allow him to have his way with her.

It was nearly midnight when they got there. The place was popular for kids wanting to make out. At first there were several cars there but they left one by one. Marie kissed Rick passionately and he caressed her breasts. After the others left she claimed she needed some fresh air.

"What the hell for?" Rick exclaimed, "We were just getting it on!"

"Oh come on," Marie laughed, "Don't be a party pooper. We have all night." Reluctantly Rick got out of the car and they walked to the edge of the rocky bluff. "Aren't the lights of Grand Junction beautiful?" she asked.

Rick could care less but he nodded yes. He reached for Marie and she kissed him and put her tongue deeply into his mouth. "You never did that before!" he cried, his excitement evident.

Marie broke his embrace and walked even closer the edge. He followed her closely until she turned around suddenly and with all her strength pushed him over the edge. She heard him scream and then there was a thud and everything was quiet. Marie shuddered; had she actually killed a man? Reality took over and she knew she had to get out of there before anyone came. She left his car there and walked the three miles back to town.

By the time she got home she was exhausted and her feet were blistered. There was a light on in the living room so she knew her mother was waiting up for her. Marie closed the door softly, took the shoes off her sore feet and looked into the living room. Her mother was sound asleep in the recliner, snoring quietly.

Marie soundlessly climbed the stairs to her bedroom, put on her night shirt and went to bed. She hadn't gone to sleep when her mother opened the door and looked in. Marie turned over with a groan and her mother was satisfied that she was asleep. She had no idea when she came home.

Each day Marie looked at the paper but Rick's body hadn't been found. If it had, half the town would have grieved for the man they thought he was.

CHAPTER

56

Two days later some hikers spotted a body lying at the bottom of the bluff and called the chief. But when they searched the entire area no body was found. "I guess those guys were seeing things," the deputy said to his partner as they walked to the squad car.

Unbeknown to the deputies, Rick had fallen on a ledge out of the area they were looking in. He hugged the bluff and held his breath when they were close, afraid they would find him. But as far as he could tell, he had a broken arm and left ankle. He thought it would be possible to crawl up the steep incline.

Rick cursed the thought of the bitch that had done this to him. He would stalk her until he had the chance to beat the life out of her. Better yet, he would hire a hit man he knew to do the job. That way it couldn't be traced to him.

It took Rick hours to reach the top because he was moving so slow. His ankle was swollen to twice its normal size and his arm was bent backwards at the elbow. Between both of his injuries, he was in horrible pain and knew he needed to see a doctor at once.

Once he reached the top of the bluff, Rick hobbled to his car on one leg. He had to drive with the opposite foot because the ankle on his right leg was broken. His doctor was on Clark Street, with steps leading up to his office that Rick had to negotiate to get up there. He had broken into a sweat and had a pounding headache.

The receptionist didn't look up when he hopped through the door. "I'm sorry but the doctor is very busy today and he can't see you until tomorrow," she said.

Rick was stressed out and lost his temper. "To hell he can't see me today! I can't wait until tomorrow!" he yelled.

The receptionist looked up, "Oh, Mr. Rayburn it's you! Of course the doctor will see you." She looked him over and asked, "What happened to you? You didn't get in another accident did you?"

"In a way," Rick growled. "I went hiking and lost my footing. I fell down the hill like a rock." The woman could see he was in a great deal of pain. She pressed a button and the doctor hurried out. He saw Rick and knew he wouldn't make his tee time. He swore that every time he wanted to relax something happened.

"Come in," he said to Rick. He hobbled into the examination room and with an effort sat on the table. The doctor looked over the ankle injury and even though it was bruised and swollen, he told him it was a bad sprain, not a break. "Sometimes a sprain takes longer to heal than a break. You'll have to use crutches for a while."

Next he checked out Rick's arm. There was crack in the bone near the elbow. "This could have been worse, but you'll still have to be put in a cast."

"Ok," Rick said. He knew his injuries would be the talk of the town. He admitted to himself that he was prone to accidents and knew he'd lose limitless hours of work. He wished he had some of his money left to tide him over.

CHAPTER
57

Murphy stopped to interview Tracy on the chief's orders. He knocked at the door and she answered it, "Hi Murphy, I didn't expect to see you! Why don't you come in, it's scorching hot out there."

He took off his hat and followed her into the house, breathing a sigh of relief. "The AC feels good!"

"Sit down please. I'll get you a cool drink. Soda, iced tea or beer, take your pick."

"Thanks, but what I'd really like is just a nice, cool glass of water."

Tracy went into the kitchen and brought Murphy a glass of water in a tall tumbler filled with ice and a slice of lemon floating on top. Murphy took a long drink and smiled at her. She was a little weathered looking but she still was pretty and didn't look her age.

Tracy sat down on the sofa. "What can I do for you detective?"

"I want to pick your brain. Perhaps you can tell us something about Rick that we don't know."

"All I can think of is that he's an SOB."

Murphy grinned. "That we know."

"Secondly, a year ago he had scads of money, but when I checked our bank accounts there wasn't any money in either of them."

"You said he had a lot of money?"

"Yes but he spent it like water. As you know he bought this beautiful house and an expensive new car. When we went out to dinner he gave excessive tips. It was nothing for him to leave a fifty dollar bill for a tip on a seventy-five dollar meal. Then after his two accidents he suddenly changed. Rick didn't give me any money for groceries and the lights were shut off for non-payment. I had to call my father for money. I expect him to come up here hopping mad. You don't know him. When he tells someone to squat, they shit." Tracy clapped her hand over her mouth. "Oh, I'm sorry, I never talk like that! What I meant to say is he's very influential, he has connections everywhere."

"When he gets here send him to see the chief. We could use his help," Murphy said, tongue in cheek. After that he left, realizing he hadn't found out a thing he didn't already know. He would go to the station and report to the chief. It was apparent to him that the investigation had stalled and he had no idea where they would go from there.

CHAPTER

58

Marie couldn't believe Rick had survived the fall, but couldn't help but be glad he had some injuries and that he was using crutches. When she went to work she told Ellen how she felt.

Ellen didn't laugh, but warned Marie that she needed to worry about how he was going to retaliate. "You know he will try to hurt you again. I think you should stay somewhere else for a while. Rock and I would love it if you would come and stay with us."

"I can't leave Mom alone."

"Think about it Marie; Rick doesn't have any gripe with her. It's you he'll be hunting down."

"I don't think he'll do anything stupid."

"Wake up! He's very vindictive."

"What can I do to protect myself?"

"I told you this before, don't go anywhere alone. I also think you should take a different route to work every day. I'll make sure you will never be left alone here and I'll be here to close up at night."

"Geez, do you really think all that is necessary?"

"Yes, and don't you forget it!"

"Alright Mom," Marie said unhappily.

"It won't last forever."

"Why?"

"I just have a feeling everything will be over soon. Rick is an impatient man."

Marie shook with fear. She knew Rick was capable of anything. Until Ellen told her about his past she wouldn't say a bad thing about him. She had realized how naive she had been before. For the hundredth time she wished she could erase that part of her life.

CHAPTER

59

Rick arranged to meet Jimmy at seven o'clock. He only knew his name; it was all the man that had referred him would tell him. All one had to do is to call a number and ask for the hit man, and the meeting was arranged. If you tried to contact the man again the recording would tell you that the number wasn't in service.

Rick agonized how he could get the five thousand dollar down payment and another five after the deed was done. As a last resort he stole some money from the bank he worked for. He told himself he would pay it back later. Then he decided he would fake a break in, and it would keep him from having to pay it back. He felt like he was a genius for devising such a plan. Now all he had to do was put the plan in action.

Jimmy whistled as he followed Marie. He had five grand in his pocket, a well-oiled gun and an adrenaline high because he was on the hunt. He lived for this and the rush he got from killing.

When Marie pulled her car over to the curb and parked, he raised his gun and got her in the sights but suddenly she ran in to Solar Realty. "I've got to be more vigilant," he scolded himself. He had missed a great opportunity to finish the job. But it was broad daylight and it was too risky to kill at that time of day. Jimmy laid the pistol down on the seat and settled in for a long wait.

An hour later the door opened and Ellen walked out. Jimmy leaned forward and looked out the window. If she was leaving, Marie would be alone in the office and the rest would be a piece of cake.

Things were never that easy. Ellen walked to her car that was parked by the side of the building and came directly back to the agency carrying her briefcase. The rest of the day was uneventful and boring. Several times Jimmy had caught himself dozing off. I'll go home and catch a quick nap and continue this surveillance later, he thought.

Jimmy turned on Thirty-Fourth Street, but turned around realizing he was heading for the last place he had stayed. He could have kicked himself for being so stupid. In his business it was mandatory that he change addresses every month. He couldn't become friends with anyone or be a frequent customer at any watering hole. Jimmy longed to go in a corner bar for a beer and chat with others, but he couldn't. It was a lonely life.

Jimmy jerked awake and sat up in bed. The alarm clock read seven o'clock and he had overslept. Now he was late. He'd made two mistakes that day. He chastised himself because he had to be alert at all times. He was acting like a novice which could get him killed.

The hit man started the day by cleaning and checking his AK47 to have it ready in case he had to make a long range shot. When he left he put it in the back seat of the car, well within easy reach.

He drove to the street where Marie lived, and parked across from her house. After two hours of watching the place, Marie walked out at the usual time she left for work. He grabbed his rifle and waited for a clear shot. Before he could fire, Marie's mother came out of the house and joined her daughter, obstructing his view. He put the AK down and swore because now he would have to wait again to shoot her.

He followed them and to his surprise they parked at the Realty office and walked in. Suddenly he could see what their plan was. Someone would accompany her everywhere she went. Because of this the hitman's job would be much harder. He figured this five thousand was used up and considered going into hiding and screw the agreement. But it was too late.

The organization that he worked for was ruthless and would eliminate him without thinking about it. Jimmy was sure they were members of the Mafia; they were powerful and would never get caught. They had eyes everywhere, and knew everything. The hit men were completely under their control. Some of the other killers in the organization had disappeared and never had been seen again. He shuddered and knew he had to do this job and do it fast or he would end up dead just like the others.

Jimmy followed Marie's car to a bank and entered the lot. When she got out, she had a bank bag clutched in her hand, obviously was making a deposit. It was clear to him she was doing her job as usual. He quickly deducted that she should be returning to the agency. Her mother was with her so she wouldn't be alone all day. He would again have to wait until the night to erase her. The clock was ticking away and it made him nervous.

The next night after work, a girl picked up Marie at about nine o'clock and took her to a popular club. He followed and watched the two of them get out and go into the bar. He had a straight shot, until a group of guys came out laughing and singing, obviously drunk.

The only thing he could do was go in and see what had transpired. The place was swinging and loaded with people. Because there weren't any seats at the bar, the two women sat down at the only empty table. The waitress took their order and came back with the drinks. Shortly, two men joined them and they spent the evening dancing with them.

When it was time for them to leave, Jimmy was on alert. He would finally have a chance to act and get away.

The two couples left arm-in-arm and his hope faded. "Damn-it to hell," he swore. What he didn't know was that the two men were undercover cops. He had just gotten in his car when his cell phone rang. "Yo," he answered.

A man's hoarse voice asked loudly, "Did you get it done?"

"No, I can't get her alone. She's always with someone and I can't get a clear shot," he answered apologetically.

"You have one day or it's over," the man warned. Jimmy knew exactly what he meant.

"Consider it done," he answered shaking.

"It better be," the man on the other end of the line growled.

"You have my word," the hit man said but found he was talking to a dead line.

Marie dropped the detectives off two blocks from the police station then drove home. Jimmy watched the two girls go into her house and after a while the other woman left.

Now is my chance, he thought and got out of the car. He crouched down and ran across the street. A light was on in the back of the house, so he walked between Marie's house and the neighbors, where it was completely dark. When he rounded the corner, he could see the room with the light on. He rejoiced! He was in luck! The window was uncovered, the blinds rolled up.

Marie was getting undressed. Instead of shooting her, he was fascinated, wanting to see her body. He hesitated just enough for her to walk away from the window. When she appeared again Marie had on a nightgown, ready to go to bed.

Jimmy took the opportunity to get the gun out of his pocket. He fired. The window shattered, causing the bullet to go wide. He fired two more times. One bullet hit the wall and fell onto the floor. The other hit a small over-stuffed chair and embedded itself into the cushion. "Jesus Christ!" he cried to himself. He'd failed again.

The neighbor's light went on and he could hear people hollering as he ran by. He had just gotten in the car when he heard sirens and saw a police car racing down the street. It stopped in front of the house and Marie met them at the door.

The gunman quickly started the car and slowly drove away. No way would the deputies think he was involved, they were too busy questioning her. Jimmy drove to the interstate, drove about five miles then pulled off onto a narrow black-topped county road. He was getting the hell out of dodge.

CHAPTER

60

Marie called Ellen at home crying. She was sure she and Rock were sleeping because the phone rang and rang. Finally Rock answered; his voice thick from sleep. "Who's calling?" Marie's voice was shaky as she said, "I got shot at!"

Rock was fully awake now. He shook Ellen, "Wake up, wake up!" he hollered.

She was awake as soon as she saw the telephone in his hand. "Who is it?" she asked knowing something was wrong. Who would call so late at night?

"It's Marie, she's been shot at!" Rock returned.

Ellen sat up in bed. "What? Where is she?"

"I didn't ask; here take the phone."

Ellen asked, "Where are you?"

"At home," Marie answered.

Ellen could tell she was scared to death. "Rock will pick you and your mother up, you can't stay there." She gestured to Rock and he got out of bed and quickly got dressed. He was out the door in minutes.

Ellen called the chief, but of course he already knew. What had happened she wondered? She told the chief that Marie would be safe at her house but suggested that a deputy patrol that area. The chief readily agreed and said he would send Deputy Helen Bosworth that was a large woman that could handle the situation.

The chief and Murphy sped to Marie's house as soon as they were alerted of the situation, it was imperative they talk to her at once.

Deputy Helen Bosworth accompanied them to be sure Marie and her mother, were physically and emotionally alright. Lillian had been in bed at the time the shooting took place and the shots fired woke her.

The chief was positive the shooter was long gone. All hired hit men had the same MO. He told Rock to take Marie and Lilian home with him for the night. He would have officers posted at the house to keep it safe and make sure there wasn't any more problems. Ellen went to work as usual in the morning, even though she was afraid to. "You go to work too," she said to Rock. "The chief told me we should go on with our normal schedules and routine. That way the gunman won't have any idea Marie is here."

Later in the day, Rock and Ellen took Lilian back to her house. All the windows were fixed and new locks were put on the doors so they felt she would be safe. Lillian's good friend, Ella Perkins will come to stay with her until this was all over with.

Marie told her mother that she was going to a convention with Ellen in New York and this is why she was packing clothes to take with her. She kissed her Mom good-bye and said she'd call her soon. The three of them drove back to Ellen's house to try to resume a normal schedule.

Ellen called her friend Tracy to cancel their lunch date for the next day and to tell her what had happened to Marie.

The news of what happened at Marie's house spread like wildfire. The neighbors and citizens of the town panicked, not knowing what had caused the episode. The situation was serious, because the chief didn't say a word, nor was there any mention of what had happened in the Chronicle.

CHAPTER

61

Ellen got home from work late the next day because she didn't have Marie at the office to help her. After a long day, it was great to walk in the door and smell food cooking. Tonight Marie was making dinner, "I appreciate your thoughtfulness, where did you learn to cook so well?" Marie told her it was her mother who learned to cook from her grandmother. Her German family often made roast pork and dressing or chicken and dumplings. Ellen thought it was a way of repaying them for letting her stay there. She also did the laundry and kept the house cleaned.

Two weeks went by and no one showed up to hurt Marie. Either the culprit didn't know where she was or he was long gone. After another week went by, Ellen decided Marie could go back to work with her. They both were delighted because Ellen needed the help and Marie was bored with staying at home.

Her first day back was hectic, and Marie was exhausted. She ate dinner and went directly to bed. The next morning, she thanked Ellen and Rock for their hospitality but told them it was time to move back home. Her mother was getting on in years and she shouldn't live alone. Ellen hated to see Marie go, she was such a sweet girl and very helpful. However, she would see her every day at work and could keep tabs on her.

When Marie got home the house was a disaster. Newspapers were scattered about the living room, there were dirty dishes in the sink and the smell of kitchen garbage filled the air. If this was any indication, her mother hadn't left the house for weeks.

She opened the refrigerator and there was only a carton of sour milk, spoiled tomatoes and a container of soup. Another two dishes had moldy food in them but there were a few eggs and some stale bread. Marie looked outside at the garden that was her mother's pride and joy and the flowers were drooping like they hadn't been watered in a week.

She ran upstairs to her mother's bedroom and found an emaciated woman lying in bed. Her body was so small it looked like a skeleton was under the covers. Marie went to the bed and gently shook her. "Come on Mom, get up! I'll fix you something to eat."

Her mother's eyes lit up when she saw Marie and she was overcome with emotion. Why hadn't she come to see her she wondered? Guilt washed over Marie as she realized she was too wrapped up in her own problems and had only thought of herself. How could she have been so selfish?

She made scrambled eggs and the tube of Grands biscuits she'd found in the refrigerator drawer. After they ate, she helped her mother into the recliner and covered her with an afghan so she could watch her soap operas. "I'm going to the store," Marie told her, "You'll be alright won't you?"

Her mother nodded and sounded like her old self by saying, "Why not? You haven't been around and I managed." Marie left without a reply.

After Mom had showered, Marie tucked her into a clean bed and then stayed up until midnight cleaning the house. Loads of dirty dishes had accumulated, the floors all needed washing or vacuuming and then there was the dusting.

Marie was exhausted but her mind was working overtime. What could she do about her mother? She wasn't able to be with her all day because she had to work.

When Ellen handed Marie her paycheck she just stared at it. There was no way she would have enough money to get her mother help at home and a nursing home was out of the question. Marie stood in one spot so long, looking at the piece of paper that Ellen thought she must want a raise. "I can't give you a raise right now. I paid you for all the time you missed."

"I appreciate it! That's not it, I don't want a raise but I haven't got enough money to take care of Mom."

Marie looked so sad that Ellen felt sorry for her. She walked over, put her arms around Marie and gave her a hug. "It will be alright," she said rubbing her back.

"No, it won't," Marie cried.

When Ellen went home that night, Rock was waiting for her with a glass of wine. "Why don't you sit down and relax for a while? I made dinner tonight," he said proudly.

Ellen smiled, "What did you make?"

"Hamburgers, frozen french-fries, and canned baked beans."

Ellen wanted to laugh but instead she praised him. "Gee thanks honey. It's great to come home and have dinner made!"

Rock wiggled his butt just like Rusty did. He rubbed his hands eagerly. "Come on, let's go."

"Can't it wait a minute? I have something to talk to you about and I want to finish my wine."

Rock looked disappointed but he sat down again. "What important thing have you got to tell me?"

"It's about Marie. Her mother is frail and she doesn't make enough money to hire someone to stay with her, much less put her in a nursing home."

Ellen sighed, "I really can't help her; we're coming into the slow season now. I wish I could."

Rock frowned. Should he tell her? Yes he would. "Why don't we ask Ella Perkins if she'd like to do it? Her husband just died and I don't think she can live on her social security."

"What a great idea! I'll talk to her tomorrow."

Ellen quit talking and frowned. "But who will pay her?"

"I will," he replied firmly.

"You make good money but not enough to do that."

"Yes, I do," he winked.

Ellen looked at him puzzled. "Here we go again," she said, "Please tell me where you're going to get it."

Rock ignored her question. "You see if Mrs. Perkins is interested, we could offer her three hundred, fifty dollars a week, and I bet she'd jump at the chance."

"You're keeping something from me and I don't like it. I don't know about you, but I'm going to eat," she said and walked toward the kitchen. What isn't Rock telling me? she wondered.

The next day Rock went to one bank and drew out fifty thousand dollars. This money will last me quite a while he thought. If it runs out there's more where that came from.

Ellen asked Mrs. Perkins if she would like the job. "I'd be delighted. I know Lillian is a good person and I think it would be good for both of us. I can stay in her spare room, like I did before. If she would like to give it a try, we'll get together." Ellen was glad to hear that, it was a good solution, especially because they knew and liked each other!

Ella Perkins fit right in at Lillian's home. Marie was delighted that her mother was flourishing now that she was there. She didn't stay in bed any longer and because Ella cooked her meals for her, she was putting on some weight.

One day Marie came home from work and Ellen and her mother were playing gin-rummy and they were talking and laughing. Marie believed a miracle had happened. The only thing that continually bothered her was that Rock was paying Ella's salary. And Marie wasn't happy about the idea of accepting charity. Somehow, some way, she would find a way to repay him.

CHAPTER

62

Ellen and Rock planned to get married a month from the time they got engaged. She selected Marie to be maid of honor and Tracy to be her bridesmaid.

Rock picked two men he worked with at JR Richards Plumbing, Walt his partner who was about his age and Charlie his supervisor who was several years older.

Since there was a beautiful green lawn behind their cottage, they decided to hold the ceremony there. After the service was over a reception was held at the Grand Junction town hall. Only fifty guests attended the wedding itself because if Ellen invited one of her clients, she would have to invite them all.

Ellen wore an ivory satin dress with a sweetheart neckline. The bodice was sprinkled with tiny white pearls and she wore a single large pearl earring in each ear. Her attendants wore light blue satin dresses, pearl jewelry and carried white flowers.

Rusty had a white bow-tie around his neck and wore a little black vest. He followed the couples, carrying a white basket trimmed with blue and white ribbons, bearing the rings for the ceremony.

Rock wore a white tuxedo with a black cumber-bun and his attendants wore black tuxedos. Everyone in the wedding party was exceptionally good looking, one person complimenting the other.

The informal reception was a blast. A three piece rock band played and the young people gyrated to the beat. The older folks watched, swaying in place and they all clapped when the musicians finished.

Ellen was cutting the cake when there was a commotion. Rock turned to see what was going on and saw Rick elbowing his way through the crowd. A guest stood his ground, not moving and Rick punched him, breaking his nose, spattering blood all over the man's clothes. Rock's jaw tightened as he looked at Ellen and said, "Look who crawled out of the woodwork."

"Get him out of here!" she cried.

Walt, the best-man, overheard the couple's words and exclaimed, "I'll gladly do it!"

After the fiasco, the reception broke up. The mood of the crowd changed and no one felt like having fun anymore. The people exited the hall quickly.

Ellen broke into tears. "Everything was so perfect until he showed up!"

Rock put his arms around her and kissed her lightly on the lips. "We won't let Rick spoil it. After all, we have the rest of the night to celebrate."

In truth, Rock's mind was churning. "I'll kill the ass-hole," he thought, but quickly stopped himself. There had been too much killing already. He would find some other way to hurt him, one that would get rid of him forever.

CHAPTER

63

The chief went over and over the things that had happened years ago in the Brink's truck robbery. The case had been re-opened but he hadn't made any arrests. The chief called Murphy into his office to go through the facts they had. Both Sam and Jason's deaths smelled of murder. The chief couldn't help but think the three cases were tied together.

Out of four, the only two poker players left were Rick and Rock. Both the chief and Murphy knew that Rock was more stable and obeyed the law and they couldn't shake the feeling that he had taken the fall for someone else. They knew Rick was involved somehow.

Murphy stopped reading the information the chief had written down and slapped his forehead. "Chief," he said loudly, "I forgot to give you the heads up on something."

"What's that?" the chief asked while he kept looking at the list in front of him.

"Rick is back!" Murphy shouted.

The chief's head snapped up and he stared at his deputy. "What did you say?"

"Yup, he crashed Ellen and Rock's wedding yesterday. Everybody freaked out and left the reception."

The chief stood up, "Let's get a move on. We have to nab this guy while we can. We'll get the truth out of him one way or the other."

Murphy didn't like the sound of that. He wasn't into torture and he didn't think the chief was either. He thought of calling in the FBI but knew the boss wouldn't have it. He wanted to solve this case himself.

Murphy put his hat on as the two men rushed out the door to find Rick and bring him in. They had no idea where he was, but come hell or high water they would find him!

CHAPTER

64

The hitman was several states away and breathing easier. Jimmy was proud of himself for getting away clean, so he wanted to celebrate, to toast himself for being so clever. He opened the glove compartment, got out a pint of vodka, and took a huge swig. It tasted so good, he took another. He was only a few miles down the road when he spotted a wayside where he could relieve himself.

Jimmy parked in front of the restrooms and got out of the car. A car door slammed and he heard someone running behind him. He laughed, thinking someone really was in a hurry and could imagine a guy losing control and peeing in his pants.

Someone grabbed his shirt collar and pulled it tight. The hitman made a choking sound as his oxygen supply was cut off. "You have something that belongs to me. Did you think you could get away with stealing my money?" a gruff male voice asked.

Jimmy grunted, not being able to reply. The cloth around his neck was pulled so tight that he coughed as he tried to pull away. Finally his body was compromised and he fell to the concrete. Jimmy's hand clutched his bruised throat as he looked up at his attacker. "Who are you?" he croaked.

The man snarled, "Give me my money!"

"I only have part of it," Jimmy whined.

"Get it, and I mean now!"

Jimmy got up and ran as fast as he could to his car where he retrieved three thousand dollars from under the driver's seat.

The attacker counted the money then punched him so hard his head flew back "Get out of my sight and remember you owe me. You can give me an IOU for the two thousand and you have a month to pay me back. If you don't, you know the consequences."

Jimmy knew. "Where will you be so I can get ahold of you?" he asked. In reality he had no idea where he would get the money.

"I'll call you," the man replied and walked away.

In a few minutes Jimmy heard a truck start and drive away. He was shaking like a leaf but made it back to his car. He knew he'd gotten mixed up with the wrong crowd and he should have known they would find him. They had contacts everywhere.

CHAPTER

65

Tracy and her father sat down in the living room after dinner. Horace said they needed to talk. Upstairs they could hear Rick moving around in his room. He was swearing and sounded like he was kicking things over. Horace started the conversation. "Did you hire investigator Barnes like I recommended? What did he find out about that nut upstairs?"

Tracy shook her head no. "I hired another one. I gave him a down payment out of the money you gave me. To make a long story short, after he found out Rick was cheating on me with a young girl, I let him go. After all, he found out all I wanted to know."

"Barnes is the best; you should have used him. He is tight-lipped and no one would know what cases he is working on."

"What's done is done," Tracy answered without regret. Then she changed the subject. "What is my brother up to now?"

"God only knows. I haven't heard from him in six months. He goes from job to job. For a long time I bailed him out of the jams he got himself into, but I finally gave up. He's a fuck-up and I'm afraid he's never going to change."

"Oh Daddy, he was such a good kid too," she cried.

"He ran with the wrong crowd."

Tracy shook her head. "I always had such high hopes for my little brother too," she sighed.

"I'll bet he's wanted by the law by now," her father said glumly.

"I doubt it, he is a loose cannon but I don't think he'd become a criminal. He's too smart for that," she replied.

Upstairs it sounded like Rick was wrecking the place. Horace said, "I'll give him a shot to settle him down," and he left the room. After fifteen minutes the loud noise stopped and it was quiet.

The next morning Horace called the chief. He explained who he was and asked the chief if they had made any progress on the cases involving Rick.

He sighed and answered, "We are sure Rick is behind it all, but we haven't any concrete evidence so far. His cell phone records prove he made many calls to Marie, as we knew. We don't have any proof he beat-up the poor girl."

Horace thought for a second then replied, "I think I can help you chief. I'll come down to the station to talk to you; I'll be there within the hour."

After Horace's discussion with the chief, he decided to let the man work with him. It just could be that he would find a new clue and the chief was excited about the prospect. He looked forward to working with Horace and Murphy as a team; they would begin at once.

CHAPTER

66

Ellen pecked Rock on the cheek then flicked her tongue in and out of his ear. At first he responded but then shoved her away. "Is something wrong?" she asked quietly.

"No," he lied, "I've just been out of sorts lately."

"Why? Is it because I'm gone so much?" Ellen worried.

"That's not it!" Rock exclaimed as he got up and walked into the living room. She followed silently and sat down on the sofa next to him.

Rock looked seriously at her. "I have something to tell you. Something I should have done long ago."

Ellen frowned, "Before we got married we promised each other there wouldn't be any secrets between us."

"That means now and in the future, not what's happened long ago in the past."

"Why tell me now? What's past is past." Some things are better left unsaid."

"Because I love you, and the truth is tearing me apart."

Ellen placed her hand over his. "You know you can tell me anything. We're soul-mates, aren't we?"

"Didn't it ever occur to you that Lillian is too old to be Marie's mother?"

Ellen thought about it then replied, "No, I've only seen the woman once or twice."

"Believe me, she's at least seventy-five years old."

"What are you getting at Rock?"

He cleared his throat and began speaking. Here goes, he thought. "Lillian is her grandmother," he said nervously.

"Who is her mother then, or father for that matter?"

"Her mother was Lillian's daughter, Laura. I'm the father."

"You mean you are Marie's father?" she screamed. "Am I the last one to know? I must be the laughing stock of everyone!" Ellen cried and tried to run from the room.

Rock caught her and held her in his arms. "Please sit down, I'm not finished," he begged. Ellen quieted and let him lead her back to the sofa. When the two of them were seated again, he explained, "No one knows besides Lillian and me. Laura died giving birth to Marie so naturally Lillian raised her. That is why I offered to pay for Mrs. Perkins to stay with her."

"That still doesn't explain your part in this. Please enlighten me!" Ellen said sarcastically.

"I told you it was a long time ago. We lived next door to each other; Laura and I played together since we were four years old. When we became teen agers both of us were curious about sex, so we began to experiment. One thing led to another and she became pregnant. Neither of us knew what to do, so we kept it a secret until Laura told her grandmother. Wisely, Lillian sent her to her sister's in St. Louis to have the baby. Children born out of wedlock were treated like cast-outs all their life. It wasn't at all like it is now. Thank God for the change."

Ellen had listened quietly to the story and her heart went out to Rock. "You should have told me earlier!" she said flatly.

"Would it have made any difference?"

"Yes, we could have done more for Lillian and Marie."

"No. Lillian is a proud woman and refused my help. I have arranged for Marie to receive three hundred thousand dollars when I die."

Ellen jumped up, staring at Rock. "Alright big boy, tell me where you are getting all this money. I'm tired of your secrets. Tell me now, or I swear I'll leave you!"

"You can't, we love each other!" Rock hollered.

"Then tell me, now!"

"The robbery was Rick's idea. Somehow I got sucked into driving the get-away car and you know the rest. The others saw that I took the rap. At least they were fair enough to give me my fair share of the take."

Ellen looked at the beautiful rings sparkling on her finger. She took them off and tried to hand them to Rock. "These were purchased with dirty money, I can't wear them," she yelled.

Then Rock raised his voice. "I sure as hell earned the money. Remember, I spent ten lousy years in prison."

Ellen reconsidered and placed the rings back on her finger. "Promise me one thing," Ellen said, "That you won't use any of the money personally, but instead, give it to others that need it."

Rock nodded yes in agreement. "I intend to," he replied firmly. "I've already begun haven't I?"

Ellen didn't have anything to say to that.

CHAPTER

67

Rick's behavior was getting worse. He was completely uncooperative and his appearance looked altered. He was wild-eyed and acted like he was out of his mind.

"My dear," Horace said to Tracy, "We have to do something about Rick, he is dangerous. For your safety, we should have him committed."

"But he's the father of my children!" Tracy exclaimed and covered her eyes with her hands, tears threatening.

"Your children will be back from summer camp soon and you don't want them to see their father in this condition, do you?"

"Nooo," she returned.

"Well then, we have to do something immediately. You must accept what Rick has become and that he needs help. Tomorrow I'm going down to the station and speak to the chief anyway. Maybe he can tell me what we should do about him," Horace said grimly.

Horace was up early and down to the station by eight am. As luck would have it, the chief agreed to see him immediately. "Mr. Carlson, It's so nice to see you again; please sit down. Let's get to the chase. Why do you feel you are qualified to help with this investigation?"

"It's a long story, but here goes," Horace answered and began, "When I was in law school I needed some money to get by. There was an ad in the paper for a delivery person. I called the number listed and had an interview. I got the job and it worked well around my classes. For six months I carried a package to many stores, and there I received a package to take back to the company I worked for. At first I didn't ask any questions, but later I wondered just what I was delivering. I carefully steamed open one package I was to deliver and found it was full of heroin. It was obvious to me that the package I took back was payment for the drugs. I immediately tendered my resignation and was called into the manager of the firm's office. He was a broad shouldered man that smoked a cigar and looked like a tough guy no one would mess with. Not wasting any words, he asked bluntly, "Why are you leaving?"

"I found I can't handle both studying and working your job too."

"You're a liar too," he snapped. "You've figured out what you're delivering, didn't you?"

I didn't know what would happen if I didn't tell the truth. "Yes," I said.

"We will forgive you if you do as we say; and believe me, you don't want to know the alternative," he advised.

"I was beginning to get the picture and realized I had inadvertently fallen into the mafia's hands. The only way I got out unscathed was that I promised when I graduated from college as a full-fledged lawyer. I would only handle their cases. I couldn't refuse or pay the consequences so I hung out my shingle and did as they instructed. The money was good because I got them out of many scrapes. After I turned sixty, I retired. End of story," Horace concluded.

"So you still have connections to the mafia," the chief stated. It was not a question.

"I am in their good graces at this time. I've given your situation a lot of thought and I am positive Marie's beating and the shots fired at her smell of a hit man," Horace explained.

"Let's say you're right, then who hired him?" The chief asked, but then answered his own question, "Rick has the only reason."

"Agreed, let's get to the next problem. He is losing it and is going to hurt himself or someone else soon."

"We have to pick him up at once. For the time being, we'll confine him at the Greyson Institution so he can get the therapy he needs. The psychiatrists there will question him in depth and use hypnotism in the hope he will confess his involvement. Then he would remain confined until the time he was ruled competent to stand trial, to face his criminal charges." The chief turned to Horace, "Welcome aboard!"

CHAPTER

68

When Marie came home from work, Rock and Ellen's car was in the driveway. How nice of them to come visit her mother she thought and ran into the house to see them. Instead of the comradery she expected to find, there was tension in the room. Her mother looked upset, while Rock and Ellen looked stern. Ellen's mouth grimaced when she tried to smile. "Come in honey," she invited quietly, trying to hide the nervousness she felt.

"Sit down with us, Marie," Rock said, "We have something to tell you."

Marie clearly didn't know what was going on, so she sat down with a dismayed look on her face, looking from one person to another, seeking an answer.

Lillian broke the silence. "I should have told you this a long time ago. I love you very much, but I am your grandmother not your mother. My daughter Laura is your mother."

A kaleidoscope of emotions reflected on Marie's face but she said nothing. Lillian got up and pulled a picture from a desk drawer and handed it to Marie. "This picture has yellowed with age, but this is your mother. It was taken shortly before she died."

Marie's hand trembled as she looked down at the pretty, blonde, young woman in the photo. It was like looking into a mirror; the resemblance was unmistakable. "Where is she now?" Marie asked.

Lillian wanted to soften the words but she had no way to do it. Instead she took Marie's hand and said, "She died giving birth to you."

"Oh no!" Marie cried, "How could that happen?"

Rock spoke up, "Back then things were different, today she probably wouldn't have died. There are many new methods and testing now." He looked at Marie with kindness. "Don't fret over something you can't change my dear."

"Who is my father then? Why didn't he take care of me?" she asked indignant.

Now is the time Rock thought and was afraid to say, "I was too young and didn't have the means to take care of you. It was Lillian's and my secret. Ellen didn't know until a few days ago either."

No one in the room would have expected Marie's reaction. She flew over to Rock and threw her arms about him and gave him a kiss on the cheek. "I am so lucky to have you as a father!" she exclaimed and even though she was a grown girl she sat on his lap and put her head on Rock's shoulder.

"I think this calls for a celebration," Ellen said.

Lillian added, "I have a bottle of Mogen David in the cupboard. I use it for medicinal purposes of course, but I'll go get it." With a grin and a wink she left the room only to return with four cordial glasses filled with wine. Everyone toasted each other and the atmosphere was like New Year's Eve, welcoming in a new future.

CHAPTER
69

It was time for the auditors from the Federal Banking Commission to examine the records of the Grand Junction Community Bank. Two men arrived early in the day, hoping they would be through with the audit in one morning. The bank had always been right on target, balancing perfectly so they expected it to be the same this time.

The men checked the figures; the deposits and withdraws three times but the totals always came out the same. Ten thousand dollars was missing!

They asked to see the manager but were told he was on sick leave. A thorough investigation would ensue. The chief and his deputies would be asked to keep up with the audit investigation and the interviewing of each employee. Everyone was cleared, with the exception of Rick.

Rick was the only one left so the investigation focused on him. The authorities agreed that because he had access to all monies and all locked areas of the bank, including the safe, that he was guilty of knowing where the missing money went.

They obtained a warrant issued by a judge for Rick's arrest. Unbeknown to them were the other criminal activities he was allegedly involved in. Both the murder of Gus and the hiring of the hitman to kill Marie.

Rick grew more and more paranoid with each passing day, falling into an even greater depression.

CHAPTER

70

The call came for Marie one morning at work. It was a hysterical Mrs. Perkins, "Oh Marie," she cried, "I came upstairs from the basement and Lillian was lying on the kitchen floor! I tried to awaken her but couldn't. She's not dead, but incoherent. I've called 911 and I'm sure they'll take her to St Paul's Hospital. Meet us there!"

Marie paced around the office until she got a grip on herself then she snatched her purse off the desk and headed for the door.

Ellen looked up wondering what was going on. She checked her watch, seeing that it was 2:15, then saw Marie's horror stricken face. "It was Mrs. Perkins; she found Lillian lying on the floor. I'm going home; I'll call you later," she shouted over her shoulder as she ran out of the building, leaving a shocked Ellen looking after her.

When Marie got to her house no one was there so she got back in her car and rushed to the hospital. She ran to the front desk and asked where Lillian Banks was. The woman checked her list of registered patients and said, "I'm sorry, but there's no one here by that name."

"She's just been brought here by ambulance. I've got to see her!" Marie insisted.

"In that case, she's probably still in the ER. Follow this hallway to the end." Belatedly she called, "Good luck!" as Marie went through the double doors.

A nurse stopped her, "No one is allowed in here!" she said firmly.

"I have to see Lillian Banks, she was just brought in!" Marie cried.

"I suggest you take a seat. We will call you when we have her ready," the woman said and hurried away. Marie reluctantly sat down and waited and waited and waited. She was getting anxious when the same nurse appeared. "I'm sorry it took so long but we had to work on her."

"What do you mean?" Marie asked frantically.

"Dr. Gross conducted CPR and used the paddle boards when her heart stopped but she remained comatose, never regaining consciousness." The nurse took her arm sympathetically, "I'm sorry but she's passed."

"Oh, My God!" Marie cried hysterically.

Ellen flew through the doors to see the scene playing out in front of her and had no doubt as to what had happened. She went over to Marie and took the inconsolable over to a chair, "Sit down and pull yourself together. Lillian had a good life; she enjoyed teaching for thirty years and has traveled most of the world. She lived to the ripe old age of seventy-five and didn't suffer."

Marie realized she was right and wiped her tears from her cheeks, "Where do I go now?" she asked, still shaken.

"I'm sure you can go back to Lillian's but if you want, you can come home with me."

"Could I? The memories would be too much right now. I wonder how Mrs. Perkins is taking it?"

"I'll bet she's a basket case. We'd better go back to the house to see her to make sure she's Ok."

The reading of Lillian's will was two weeks later. Her attorney quickly read her wishes and said that he would be contacting all the recipients. Marie drove Mrs. Perkins so she wouldn't have to go alone.

Lillian's will was full of surprises. She had accumulated a half a million dollars over a lifetime. Because she was frugal she saved much of her salary. A nephew was given a hundred thousand dollars to be used for college. Mrs. Perkins receives one hundred thousand for being a good friend, and to Marie's amazement she had left her the house. In addition fifty thousand was to go to her church and another fifty thousand to a disabled veteran's clinic. The rest was to be given to several charities such as the Guide Dogs, St Jude's Hospital and the Shriner's Hospital for children.

Things were rough for a while after Marie moved into the house. She was busy painting the walls which badly needed it. She also replaced the appliances which were very old. The only other new thing she added was a small chest freezer. She intended to keep Lillian's garden alive and flourishing in her memory, and was determined to learn to freeze the vegetables she grew.

Marie would have a drastically different life and was looking forward to enjoying every minute of it.

CHAPTER
71

Tracy was sitting at the kitchen table staring into her coffee cup when a hard knock came on the front door. The chief and his men were there to serve the warrant to Rick and pick him up.

"Hello Tracy," the chief greeted her. He noticed that her face looked pale and drawn with her wrinkles prominent. My God, she's aged ten years since he'd seen her last, he thought.

"Why are you here?" she asked, afraid of the answer.

"We've come to pick up Rick; we have a warrant for his arrest. You know we have to serve it to him in person. Where is he?"

"Please don't, please," she begged.

"The kids come back tomorrow," Horace reminded her.

"I know but…"

"Where is he?" Murphy demanded looking around the room.

"He hasn't gotten up yet, usually he sleeps until noon."

The men entered the house, looking throughout the rooms. "He's in the second bedroom down the hall on the left," Tracy moaned, as three of them went up the stairs.

The bedroom door was closed so they turned the knob to open it. They were alarmed when they saw the empty bed. After searching the closet and under the bed they deducted Rick was nowhere to be found. "Son of a bitch," the chief swore, "He flew the coup. Now we'll have to put out an APB on him."

The chief and Murphy searched the neighborhood, while Horace knocked on doors to see if anyone had seen him recently. One man who had been out walking his dog admitted that had.

"Where was he when you saw him?" Horace asked the man.

The man pointed to a street about a block away. "My dog and I got away from him as quickly as we could. What crazy person takes a walk in his pajamas in broad daylight?"

The three men spread out to broaden their search area but Rick was nowhere to be found. The chief suggested going back to the station to put together a plan to find him.

The chief just got into his office when a deputy knocked at the door. "Chief, I thought you may want to know that the report on the gun that was found in the lake is finished. The serial numbers showed the revolver to be registered to Rick Rayburn. Ballistics tests show it was last fired approximately a month ago. The remaining bullets are still in the chamber and we may be able to lift fingerprints from them. The lab is going over them now. They also are checking to see if it matches the bullet taken out of Gus's body. The gun had been reported stolen and they figured Rick had thrown it in the water to get rid of it."

"You don't say. It looks like we've found who murdered the investigator too! The evidence is now more than circumstantial. We've got Rick tied to more than one incident, and more than enough to hold him on," the chief enthused.

"Have Murphy come in here, would you?" the chief asked.

"Yeah chief," Murphy said as he came into the office.

"Let's look over the surveillance tapes from the parking garage where Marie was beaten up. The courier just dropped them off."

They concentrated on the build of the attacker. He was tall and lean with broad shoulders, indicating a man about six feet tall. The build fit Rick to a tee.

"Murphy, wasn't the accident you had with Rick only two blocks from the parking garage? What was the exact time? I'll bet Rick was just leaving the parking ramp when you smacked him. Why hadn't we thought of this before?" the chief grimaced.

The pieces of the puzzle were falling into place.

CHAPTER

72

Rick and Ellen thought Marie was lonely because she found an excuse to come over to their house every day.

"Maybe Marie should get a roommate," Ellen suggested to Rock.

"I don't think that's a good idea. She's a big girl and is old enough to live by herself. Besides, she has friends she can go places with. She could go back to school and get herself a broker's license. That would be a great help to you."

"That's a good idea but I would like for her to learn the ropes first. I can talk to her about it."

"Why not get her a puppy; someone to keep her company?"

"What a great idea!" Ellen replied. "Let's go to the pound and get her a rescue dog like Rusty!"

"It's a deal, we'll go tomorrow."

Animal Services was filled to capacity, with many cats and dogs waiting to be adopted. They walked past cage after cage with each dog standing up on their back legs, looking through the bars, watching them go by. Every one of the dogs wanted to go home with them, making Ellen feel terrible.

Finally they saw a golden retriever lying in the back of his cage. He was a puppy, but he didn't move and was shaking with fear. An attendant walked up to Ellen and Rock and said, "That poor pup just came in and he is scared to death."

"Could you get him out of the cage please?" Ellen asked.

When the dog came out he ran immediately to Ellen, and snuggled against her. She petted him and scratched him behind the ears. He wiggled all over her and Ellen fell in love. The plaque on the door said the puppy was named Rex and he was twelve weeks old. Ellen took him in her arms and he licked her face making her giggle. "Isn't he cute!" she crooned.

"Let's get out of here before you get the idea of taking a playmate home for Rusty," Rock exclaimed.

Ellen didn't say a word and stood silently as Rock paid the eighty-five dollar adoption fee. Then she broke out in a wide smile, "We'll give Rex to Marie for her birthday!" Ellen said excitedly. "I know she'll love him!"

CHAPTER

73

Horace purposely told Tracy he was going out to see an old friend. He intended to call Marrelli, who was his contact in the mafia and didn't want her to know about it.

The phone rang several times before the call was answered, "Marrelli," was all the man said.

"Carlson here."

"What do you want?" he asked shortly.

"To pick your brain for a minute," Horace said.

"Shoot."

"Did you take a request for a hitman to take out a woman last month?"

"You know better than to ask me that."

"I know I'm pushing it, but it's important."

Marrelli thought for a moment then growled, "Ok, just this one time, but don't ask again! If the boss finds out, I'll end up in a cement slab like our friend Hoffa did. Well, he's gone now but you know what I mean."

Horace asked one more question although he knew he was risking it, "Who paid you to do the job?"

"Some mucky muck, I don't even know his name. He screwed us too; he only made a down payment. But because he was who he said he was, we believed he was good for it. Big mistake, but he'll pay. And

I repeat, don't call again!" and he slammed down the phone so hard it echoed in his ear.

Horace felt sure that it was Rick and that's why he was on the run. It would kill Tracy when he was caught and put in jail, because this time he wouldn't be getting out.

CHAPTER

74

The chief's men searched high and low for Rick but he was nowhere to be found. Nor did the APB result in any sightings of him.

The chief and his new deputy Basel were patrolling a well-known high-risk area. A crowd had gathered a block away and they thought it was most likely two gangs rumbling with each other. They parked the squad car a block away and walked to the confrontation where they stopped short when they realized they were mistaken.

A man dressed in blue pajamas was standing on a chair ranting and raving. He spread his arms out and screamed, "What good have the police done for you? Everyday, youths get shot and riots occur!"

The crowd yelled back and some raised their fists in the air in agreement. "I say, take the law into your own hands!" There was loud shouting. "An eye for an eye," he yelled, and the crowd went crazy, chanting and stomping their feet.

"We've got to get this psycho off the street," the chief told his deputy. They pushed their way through the crowd, with Billy-clubs in hand. They were shoved by protestors trying to stop them. The chief raised his pistol overhead and shot it twice into the air. Some of the people were scared and ran away, but most stayed to watch the action.

It was then that Rick's dazed expression changed. He saw the cops and jumped off the chair. In his haste, the chair flew backward and hit an old man in the knees knocking him down. The incident didn't stop Rick for a minute because he knew the officers were in his pursuit.

"Don't let him get away!" the chief hollered to Basel as they both ran full tilt after Rick. They were gaining on him when a car with blackened windows skidded to a stop near them. The passenger door flew open, Rick jumped in and they raced away.

The chief stood, trying to catch his breath as he watched the car take off. "Son of a bitch!" he hollered and the crowd booed loudly at him. He gave them a dirty look and hurried back to the squad. The chief was soaked with sweat, so he used his handkerchief to wipe his brow.

When they got into the car, Basel turned up the AC to full blast. "Where the hell do you think he's off to?" the deputy asked.

"I'll be damned if I know," the chief said exasperated. "But what I do know, is that I'm stopping at the next watering hole and ordering the biggest glass of beer they have!"

"What the hell, it's five o'clock somewhere," Basel agreed.

CHAPTER

75

Jimmy was beside himself, anywhere he went the Mafia would find him. He made up his mind that he had to call the forbidden number and let the chips fall where they may. He knew his chances were slim of getting what he wanted, but he had no choice if he didn't want to end up six feet under. Jimmy's heart beat double time as he punched in the number.

An unfamiliar voice answered, "Who is this?" the man asked, his voice heavy with an Italian accent. Oh my God, it's Louie, Jimmy thought, I'm speaking to the Don himself! "Never mind, I got your number on caller ID," the man said. Suddenly his voice became ugly when he realized it was Jimmy calling, "You were told to never call here, unless it was acritical situation."

Jimmy was scared, "It is!" he wailed. The boss laughed uproariously. "Please give me one more chance," Jimmy begged. "I haven't got the money, but if I do a job for nothing, we should all be square," he said hopefully.

"I could squash you like a bug!" Louie seethed.

"Please, please," Jimmy begged, embarrassing himself.

The Don considered, then returned, "Alright you're on but this time you'd better get the job done. It's a tough one this time. I want you to take out the man who hired you. We know he and his boys pulled off the Brink's robbery. The man is stupid but he is slippery as an eel. First of all, you have to find him, which won't be easy," he warned.

"I'll do anything," Jimmy pleaded.

"Ok you're on. You know this is your last chance or you'll end up floating in Lake Michigan."

Jimmy damned sure knew that. "You can count on me, Boss," he promised.

"Yah sure," Louie said sarcastically and abruptly hung up.

Jimmy knew he had been given a reprieve but he had no idea where to locate this guy. Then came a bright idea; he thought if he told Rick to pay him the ten grand he owed him, he would be saved. He was broke and could feel the money in his hand already. Jimmy whistled as he got into his car thinking that this deal will be a piece of cake.

Now both the chief and his men were looking for Rick, and so was he. Who would find him first and come out the victor? It remained to be seen.

CHAPTER
76

Marie's little Rex was growing fast. He was a stubborn little guy and refused to obey her. She always kept a wooden spoon handy so she could threaten him with it when he was naughty. So far Rex was afraid when Marie shook it at him, but she knew he'd figure out soon that she would never hit him with it. He was too smart for his own good.

One day Rex jumped the fence when she was at work, got lost and wound up at the pound. Thankfully, Marie had called the shelter and asked them if a Golden Retriever was picked up that day. They answered, yes there was and that she could come down and pick him up. She drove like a madman the ten miles to Animal Services.

When Rex saw her, he yelped for joy. "Did you miss me honey?" Marie crooned, then stopped herself and shook her finger at him, "Bad boy," she scolded him. Rex immediately laid his ears back and looked ashamed of himself.

A volunteer let Rex out of the cage and the dog obediently followed Marie into the office where she paid the one hundred dollar fee, commenting that she couldn't afford this. She looked at Rex with disgust and said, "We're stopping on the way home and buying a chain for you, so you can't get away," she scolded him in a stern voice. Now I'm talking to a dog she thought, I must be losing my mind!

The next incident was when she'd let Rex out to play and he didn't come back when she called. She searched the back yard and didn't find him, but she did find the hole he had dug to get under the fence.

Beside herself, Marie called the pound but this time Rex wasn't there. She prayed he would find his way home and by a miracle, within an hour he was sitting on the front steps. She was so happy to see him that she hugged him tightly and didn't scold him. When Rex got in the house Marie gave him his food and water. He gobbled all the food down, drank all the water in his dish, then bolted for her bed and fell sound asleep, he was exhausted.

Where on earth could he have gone Marie wondered? Rex hadn't eaten anything that was for sure. She thought about how attached she had become to her little furry friend. After that day she locked Rex in the bathroom when she left for work. After a month of confinement, she let the dog run the house, thinking his running days were over.

A couple of months later, Rex barked furiously like he always did when someone was coming. Marie opened the door to a strange woman standing there with a small Golden Retriever in her arms.

Marie looked at the woman in confusion. "May I help you?" she asked bewildered.

The woman frowned. "Here, take her," she said and shoved the puppy in Marie's arms. "The stud fee is usually your pick of the litter but you'll have to be satisfied with her. I don't want another female dog, just look what happens." Marie noticed Rex looking at the puppy with interest. "Yeah buddy," the woman said, shaking her finger at him, "You're the daddy." She turned to Marie, "Keep your dog home or I'll report him," she threatened.

She threw her hands up in the air and said, "Oh forget it! I'm getting Daisy spayed. I should have done it before." The woman left in a huff, leaving Marie standing in the doorway, holding the puppy. Now she had two dogs!

"Look what you've done!" she shouted at Rex. "Maybe I should get you snipped, how would you like that?" Suddenly, the hilarious situation made her burst out laughing. Marie laughed so hard she cried.

There were things she must do immediately. First she would enroll Rex in obedience class at PetSmart and the puppy could go too! And she would have them both micro-chipped, so there wouldn't be any more missing dogs.

"What do I call you?" she said to the little female, "You don't have a name so I'll call you Sunshine!" she told the little golden dog.

From that night forward, the pup slept on the bed with Marie and Rex every night.

CHAPTER

77

"Great!" the chief groused to Basel and Horace. "Now both the Mafia and the authorities are looking for Rick. Do you have any idea where we can find him?" Horace shook his head and Basel agreed. "Get your thinking caps on boys. The mayor is breathing down my neck." He looked at Basel, "Here's your chance to crack your first big one, let's see how you do."

"We'll find him," Horace said confidently.

"Get to it then, the Mayor expects an arrest like yesterday!"

"We've got to show the chief what we're made of," Basel said to Horace when the chief left the room. "What should we do? Where should we look? I have no idea."

"Let's go back to the basics," Horace replied. "Where would you go if you were a wanted man?"

Basel returned, "Somewhere right under everyone's nose where we'd never look for him. What do you have in mind?"

"I have an idea, come on let's go and see." They walked to the car hoping Horace was right. "Drive over to my daughter's place," Horace instructed the deputy as they got in the car.

"Why?"

"Because I suddenly have the urge to see my daughter," Horace said and winked at him.

"What's going on, or do you want to keep me in the dark?"

"You know I'd never do that," Horace replied. "Tracy's house is in the next block, make a left turn," he directed.

When Basel parked the car and they got out, instead of going to the front door, Horace walked around the house. The deputy followed on his heels. "Where are you going? Are you going to sneak up on your daughter?"

"Of course not, we're heading for the shed." When they got there, Horace dropped to his knees and inspected some footprints that appeared to go back and forth from the shed. In a moment he got up and began walking to the house.

"What were you looking for?" the deputy asked puzzled.

"Footprints; they were a large shoe size, maybe an eleven or twelve. They're too big to be Rick's. I was sure he would come back to his home where he felt safe. Come on let's talk to Tracy, over a cup of coffee."

If there was any question about whose footprints they were, Tracy cleared it up. "Dad, they aren't Rick's. If you want to know, they belong to the man that mows the lawn. He was here yesterday." She looked her father straight in the eye. "What makes you think Rick was here?" she asked.

"Look Tracy, he's running scared and needs a safe place to hide."

Tracy was about to object but stopped abruptly. "I didn't think much of it, but when I came home from shopping yesterday the front door wasn't locked. Oh my God, do you think Rick was here?" She jumped up from her chair and ran toward the steps leading upstairs. "I'm going to see if I can find anything out of the ordinary!"

When she came back she had a pair of blue pajamas clutched in her hand. "Rick was here. Hangers are all over the closet floor and some of his clothes are missing."

"I thought he would show up. Now that he's wearing everyday clothes no one will notice him. Come on, it's not likely he'll come back here," he said to the deputy.

"Dad," Tracy called, trying to get her father's attention, "What time are you coming home for dinner?"

Horace didn't even turn around, "When you see me, you'll see me," he said. "I don't have any idea."

Tracy watched him leave and shook her head. Her Dad was acting like a dog hot on the trail of a rabbit. She knew the expression in his eyes. When he had that look it always meant he was entirely absorbed by one thing and wouldn't give up until he got what he wanted. God help Rick, she thought, he doesn't stand a chance.

CHAPTER
78

Rex was nowhere in sight. Marie called and called his name but he didn't come. So much for obedience class she thought, and was very upset.

"Hey neighbor! Don't worry, I have him," a male voice called from a handsome man's face peering over the fence. It was then that she noticed a broken slat in the fence, the siaze a dog could squeeze through. "What's his name?" he asked.

"It's Rex, what's yours?" she countered.

"I'm Steve, your neighbor."

Marie realized she'd never met the family that lived next door. "I'm sorry. I haven't met any of my neighbors yet."

"I'm going to repair this hole in the fence for you. Rex likes to come over and chase our cat."

Marie laughed, "Well, we can't have that, can we?"

"Hey, I have an idea. When do you get home from work?"

"Usually about six o'clock; give or take a little."

"How about we get a bite to eat Monday after you get home? Nothing fancy, just talk and get to know each other."

Why not Marie thought, it was time she did something else other than work. Besides, Steve looked to be about her age and seemed like he would be a fun date.

"Ok," she answered, "But I won't be ready until about six-thirty."

"Fine, I'll run over and pick you up. Here's your boy," he said, shoving Rex through the fence to her. The dog licked Marie's face with sloppy kisses and her thoughts of scolding him disappeared.

I've just met a new friend, she told Rex. He looked at her with his brown eyes, seeming to know just what she said.

Marie and Steve enjoyed their time together. They had gone to Bob Evans and had a hamburger, fries and a large piece of chocolate pie for dessert. Amongst other things, Steve told her that he'd just finished college with a master's degree in accounting. He had a job with The Wiggins Accounting Corporation, the biggest firm in town. His last name was Johnson; his mother was Gayle and his father was Tom.

When he asked Marie about her life, she didn't know what to say other than she worked at Solar Real Estate and was studying to be a broker; and that she was the only child in the family. After all, she just met the guy and wasn't sure he would understand if she told him about her affair with Rick and the baby. She explained that she'd inherited the house from her grandmother when she passed away recently.

When they got back to her house, Steve gave her a friendly peck on the cheek, said goodnight and went home. What a nice guy she thought. He was polite, easy to talk to and she looked forward to seeing him again.

Rex and Sunshine met Marie at the door. Again she reminded herself that she had to look for a good home for the dog. She was too busy to have two animals to look after.

CHAPTER

79

Rick wasn't stupid; he knew the Mafia would come after him for the money he owed. After he went home and got his clothes, he stole an old Ford from one of the used car lots. He put the plate from his totaled sports car on the back, who would know?

He drove the beater to the bank and used his key to open the back door. Rick went directly to the men's rest room, cleaned up as best he could, put on a clean pair of jeans and a t-shirt.

He decided he'd crash at the run-down motel just a few blocks from the bank. He knew it was a flop house but it was ideal for his purposes. When it was safe, he would leave the country, go to Europe, lose himself in the population there and start over. He knew neither the law, nor the Mafia would find him there.

Somehow, he'd have to get some money to make his plan work. I'll figure something out he thought. Rick didn't care if it was illegal or not. Hell, he was in so deep now, one more charge wouldn't make any difference.

CHAPTER

80

Two guys from the Mafia entered the Community bank and looked around. Nothing looked suspicious, but they wanted to be sure that Rick wasn't there.

One of the men asked a teller if the manager was in. She hemmed and hawed, but finally admitted he wasn't employed there any longer. When asked if she knew where he was, she shrugged and answered coldly, "I don't know, probably in jail, that's where embezzlers end up don't they?"

Jimmy knew Rick because he was the one who hired him to bump off Marie. He worked for the Mafia but he moon-lighted on the side too. Most of the time he was successful, but sometimes he didn't get the job done for a variety of reasons.

Rick and Jimmy had a lot in common; they both broke the law with no regrets. It was all for money, both hungered for it and would do anything to get it. So when Rick asked Jimmy to pick him up from his motel, he gladly agreed.

But now Jimmy was in a jam with the Mafia, and he couldn't find Rick to help him out. He thought they could get a house together, in a secluded area where they wouldn't be apprehended.

Both of them were on the run, so when Jimmy finally got together with Rick, he'd bring up the idea of them living together. He was sure that Rick would jump at the idea.

Finding Rick became an obsession. Jimmy shadowed the Mafia wherever they went, confident they would eventually lead him to Rick. He was very careful not to be seen because he knew they would shoot him.

One night Jimmy happened to see Rick outside a building, he was peering in the window, casing the place. Jimmy pulled to the curb a block away and hurried to the liquor store. He came up behind Rick and stuck his finger into his back yelling, "Freeze!" then grabbed his arm and turned him around.

"Oh, it's you. What the hell are you doing here? You scared the hell out of me," Rick exclaimed.

"Trying to keep you from doing something stupid, this store is small potatoes. If you're going to rob some place for money, go to somewhere you will get enough to make it worth the risk."

"But I need some cash now!" Rick whined.

Jimmy shrugged but then changed his mind. "Ok, we'll pull this job together and I'll show you how it's done."

Maybe he's right Rick thought. I planned a robbery years ago when I didn't have the slightest idea how to do it and I've been in trouble ever since.

"Follow me," Jimmy said, opening the store's door. "Hello there," he said cheerfully to the old man behind the counter who frowned at him.

"I am about to close. Please select what you want and I'll check you out," the old man said.

Jimmy's expression changed, "You're in business to make money aren't you?"

The old man checked his watch, "Look, I work long hours and I'm tired. Please get what you want so I can close up."

Jimmy leaped over the counter with an ugly look on his face. "You're pushing us around old man!" he yelled and grabbed his tie and jerked it. The man's face grew red and he began to cough. Jimmy saw the man's hand reach for the button under the counter, obviously for some alarm. He moved like lightening, jerking the man swiftly over the counter.

"Stand up!" Jimmy ordered the man.

He struggled to his feet, shaking with fear, "I'm sorry if I offended you. How can I help you?" His eyes darted side to side, finally understanding the men were not customers at all.

Jimmy motioned to Rick, "Get the cash," he directed.

Rick ran behind the counter and opened the cash register. There wasn't more than fifty bucks in it. He looked at Jimmy, "There's only a few dollars in here."

"What did I tell you?" he growled back. Then he turned to the old man, who was almost in tears, pulled out his pistol and shot him point blank in the chest. He fell to the floor without a sound and lay still.

A door in the back of the store opened and a woman began to enter, saying "George, I heard…" She stopped when she saw Jimmy still holding his gun, then screamed and tried to run back out the door. Jimmy calmly raised his arm and shot her in the back.

Rick watched the scene in horror. "Let's get out of here," he cried, starting for the front door.

"Where the hell you going, don't you get it? This is a robbery gone wrong. Take a liquor box and fill it up." Rick did as he was told, while Jimmy checked the old man's pockets. "Look what I found!" he laughed loudly and held up a fifty dollar bill.

"Let's go!" Rick urged, picking up the case of scotch. Jimmy calmly stepped over the man's body and finally walked toward the door. Then he turned around and scanned the room. "What the hell are you doing?" Rick hollered.

"You always check the scene of the crime to make sure you didn't leave any evidence behind."

Rick wrestled the liquor box to his car and placed it on the back seat. Jimmy followed him and looked at Rick expectantly. "What?" Rick asked him.

Jimmy held out his hand, "You owe me half the take."

Rick reached into his pocket where he had stuffed the bills. He counted the money and it totaled forty-eight dollars. "Here's your share, man," Rick said handing him twenty-four dollars.

"You keep it. I just got fifty bucks off the old man. Listen, I have to go. Don't spend all your money in one place!" he laughed and walked back to his car.

Rick had to prod himself to get into his car and drive away. What had just happened? He couldn't believe two people had been shot in cold blood for a lousy fifty dollars. Rick felt a delayed reaction; he was shaken to the core. How could Jimmy be so cold, so ruthless? Then he remembered who he was, after all he was a hit man. He killed for money, so it was just a way of life to him.

Rick started the car and stomped on the accelerator. He drove a few blocks then slowed down to the proper speed. A squad car, sirens wailing whizzed by on the other side of the road, probably on its way to the liquor store. Rick cut his speed and drove on down the road to nowhere. He couldn't think straight but he knew the answer was to get as far away from Jimmy as he could. He didn't have the stomach for his kind of work. Anyone that could do something like that wasn't human he thought. He never wanted to see the creep again.

Rock and Ellen's house wasn't far away so he drove to the edge of their property and parked in a thick grove of trees. Before he settled down for the night, he wanted something to help him take the edge off, to help him sleep. He opened the liquor box, twisted open a bottle of scotch and took several gulps. The liquid burned all the way down to his stomach.

He took the blanket that was lying on the floor in the back, wrapped it around his shoulders, and laid back. His foot hit the steering wheel, blowing the horn. Suddenly the lights came on in the house, then the porch light came on. "Who's there?" Rock hollered.

A large dog ran out the door and ran full-steam toward the car. When Rusty got there he circled the car and barked furiously without stopping. Rock grabbed his cell phone.

Rick rolled the window down and shouted, "Don't call the police Rock!" He saw Rock snap the phone shut. "It's just me!"

Rock called Rusty off. Rick hoped he'd go back in the house but instead he strode quickly toward him. Rick wondered what excuse he could possibly give him for being there. Rock wasn't sure if he should turn him in or not, but knew he wanted some answers from Rick. I'll wait until in the morning, he told himself and he headed back to the house.

He got up early to talk to Rick, but when he went outside, his car was gone.

CHAPTER

81

Rick filled the car up with gas, stopped at a drive-in to get some food and then he went to the laundromat to wash his dirty clothes. To his dismay, he had only had five dollars left in his wallet.

He tried to think of a place to get more money. Rob a bank? No it was too risky and besides he'd tried that already. Or should he rob the gas station at gunpoint? Rick nixed that idea because there were always too many people around. After thinking a while longer, he came up with the idea that Solar Realty kept a large sum of cash in their office. He would watch the place to see what hours they were open and would devise a plan to rob the place at night.

He will pick the lock on the back door around midnight when no one was around to see him. He also knew when the police patrolled the area so he could get in and out quickly, in between the times that they drove by.

When Rick got inside the realty office, he checked all the drawers in Marie's desk first and found nothing. But in Ellen's desk he hit the jackpot. There was a bank bag containing cash and checks. He knew better than to steal checks because he'd have to forge signatures and he would go to jail for felony forgery.

He found only three hundred dollars cash, which was better than nothing. He stuffed the bills in his jacket pocket and started down the hallway to the back door. Suddenly a search light lit up the room so he laid down flat on the floor. Fortunately the bright beam passed above him, highlighting the desks and file cabinets. The police had changed their patrol schedule. Rick wondered why, but then remembered there had been several break-ins around the area.

Rick dreamed of how he could spend the money. He hadn't had any for a month and it was already burning a hole in his pocket.

CHAPTER

82

When Ellen came in to work in the morning, she immediately knew something was wrong. Her desk drawer was partially open and a few envelopes had fallen on the floor. She looked further and discovered all the cash was missing from her bank bag, but no checks were taken. She decided to call the police.

Murphy had served his time in the office and was happy to be back at his regular duties, so he and the chief responded to her call. "How much money are you missing?" Murphy asked Ellen.

"Three hundred dollars," she replied and knew by the look on the chief's face that she shouldn't have said that.

He looked around the office and said, "We'll dust for finger prints, etcetera but I'm sure this thief is smart enough to not leave any. Come on, Murphy, let's get to it." Both of the men put on gloves and began processing the crime scene. Murphy held a black light over the furniture, window sills, door handle, lock and anywhere they had dusted for prints.

The chief ascertained that the intruder had entered through the back door so he wouldn't be seen by the hourly patrol.

They both said good-bye to Ellen on their way out. "I'll call you if we find anything," the chief promised.

When Ellen got home, she couldn't wait to tell Rock what had happened. He could see that she was all worked up and wanted to talk. He gave her a quick peck on the cheek and said, "I can see you're upset about something, sit down and tell me all about it."

She told Rock about the robbery and what the chief had said. "You know, he blamed it on the fact that there has been a rash of robberies in the area. Do you think I could have been targeted?"

"Seriously, how can you think that?"

Ellen shrugged, "It's just a feeling," she said lamely.

For some reason Rick's face flashed before Rock's eyes. Why would he have come there that night? Rock hadn't told Ellen the truth about his being there. She just thought Rusty had gotten carried away barking at something outside, as he often did. Something was amiss, Rock and Rick were hardly friends anymore. Rock vowed to seek him out and find out what he was up to.

Now the Police, the Mafia and Rock were all looking for Rick.

CHAPTER

83

The Mafia was putting pressure on Jimmy to get the job done as the deadline was fast approaching. The fact was that he didn't get the thrill out of killing like he once did. Rick would be his last job then he would go underground.

Jimmy thought how foolish he had been to think he could show Rick how to rob and kill. Some men just don't have the stomach for it. He was itching to get the last job over and put his plan in motion, so he could get out of the flea bag motel he was staying at.

Jimmy spotted Rick's wreck of a car parked in front of a room and he parked next to it. He knocked on the door but there was no response. Funny, he thought, he must be there because his car was there, so Jimmy knocked even louder.

He heard a groan and a sleepy eyed Rick opened the door. "What are you doing here?" he asked angrily and tried to slam the door shut.

Jimmy put his boot in the door to keep it from closing and pushed his way into the room. He could have shot Rick right then and there, but since it was his last kill, he wanted to make him squirm a little. "Sit down!" he ordered.

Rick flopped down on the bed and stared at Jimmy. Then Rick raised his arms in the air, "Ok, get it over with!" he screamed.

"Settle down, the time isn't right."

Rick looked warily at him, "Why?"

Jimmy laughed, "I want to see you squirm first." He walked over to Rick and pulled him roughly to his feet. "Come on, we're out of here.

Ride with me and I'll bring you back to your car." He grabbed him by the sweatshirt and dragged him out to his car. Jimmy had thirty pounds on Rick so he couldn't think about getting away from him. Instead he let Jimmy shove him in the car door, and slammed it behind him.

Rick leaned back against the seat, resigned to let Jimmy take him where he would. Soon the houses looked familiar. He sat upright, "Where the hell are you going?" Rick cried.

"To take you home."

"Shit, no, why?"

"So you can kiss Tracy good-bye," he said and burst out laughing.

"You're out of your mind!" Rick protested, but by then Jimmy was turning into the driveway. Rick sat immobile in the seat.

Jimmy walked around the car and opened the door, "Are you coming or should I shoot you right here?"

"Nooo," Rick wailed. Suddenly the front door of the house opened and a man stood looking at the strange car in the drive.

"Who's there?" he called. Rick stared at the man who held a pistol in his right hand.

Suddenly Jimmy started acting strange. He tried to start the car to get out of there, but it wouldn't turn over. Rick couldn't read the strange expression on Jimmy's face as he cursed and got out of the car, ready to run.

CHAPTER

84

M arie and Steve got together every Saturday night. They became friends and she felt like she'd known him all her life. Sometimes he came over and they just sat on the porch and talked about their lives before they met. Marie couldn't bring herself to tell him the whole story about Rick and what had happened. She thought there would be time to tell him later.

Steve loved Marie's two dogs. When his cat died of old age, he took little Sunshine off her hands. To Marie's surprise, Rex moped around for a week after Sunny left. It was clear he missed her company so much that Marie gave him extra special attention until he was over it.

After a while Steve became bolder and his small kisses grew longer and more intimate. Although Marie liked him, she wouldn't let things go any further. She knew Steve was getting serious and she thought of breaking their relationship off, but didn't want to lose his friendship.

Suddenly Rick started calling her again, acting like nothing bad had happened between them. Each time Marie slammed the phone down hoping he would get the message, but his calls continued. She could tell by his voice and his erratic speech that he was losing it and she was afraid of what he might do.

Finally Marie called the chief to report the calls and asked for protection. He told her he was understaffed but would put a tap on her line, and insisted it would be monitored 24/7. He said that when Rick called her, to keep him talking, to give them enough time to find out where the call was coming from.

Marie did as the chief asked her to do and the calls stopped coming. The chief was very upset when it happened. "God damn-it!" he swore, Rick had foiled him again.

Marie told Steve that someone was calling her number and harassing her, so he came over and spent the nights with her, until they both had to leave for work in the morning.

CHAPTER

85

Rick reluctantly got out of the car. Tracy was watching the scene between Horace and Jimmy play out. Then she saw Rick and motioned him to come into the house. He wanted to go to her because this was his home and his refuge, but hesitated to do so because he was a wanted man. Finally he put his worries aside and did as Tracy wanted.

When Rick got inside, the familiarity of the place washed over him. How could he have been so foolish? Tracy led him into the kitchen where she had fresh coffee brewing. "Sit down," she instructed. "Tell me just what you've been up to. The police have been here looking for you."

Slamming car doors outside ended the conversation. She got up and ran to the window to see what was happening, with Horace right behind her.

The chief and Murphy were headed toward the house. Tracy wanted to tell Rick to hide but something stopped her. Horace watched the scenario play out before him. The chief and Murphy were talking to man he didn't know but thought the man looked familiar.

Seeing who it was, Horace hurried over to him. He hugged Jimmy and proclaimed "Hello Son," and put his arm around him. "Come into the house and see your sister. We've missed you."

Jimmy started walking toward the house but just before he got there, he ran as fast as he could around the corner of the house. Horace hollered but Jimmy didn't turn around. He just kept sprinting toward the woods behind the house.

The chief and Murphy took off after Jimmy in hot pursuit. But because they were so far behind him they stopped only to see him run into the woods and disappear. "Call for a canine," he instructed Murphy. He thought it might be too late because the man was a criminal and would know how to cover his tracks. After that they had the car towed because they knew if Jimmy didn't have wheels it would be difficult for him to get out of the area and go under. The two cops were so engrossed in catching Jimmy they completely forgot about Rick.

Rick stayed at home with Tracy and his kids where he felt secure. It only took the cops a day to realize their mistake, so they returned to Rick's home where they found him relaxing on a lounge drinking iced tea. He didn't look surprised when he saw them, but got up and turned around waiting for the chief to cuff him.

Rick rode with the chief and Murphy without saying a word. In truth, he was afraid of Jimmy and would welcome the safety of being in jail. He was sure he would be sentenced by a judge for his crimes and would accept the consequences. He was sure Tracy would lawyer him up with a good attorney.

CHAPTER

86

The chief had ignored his investigation of the liquor store for too long. Lately he and Murphy had spent all their time trailing Rick and ignoring the other cases. He called Basel in and asked him to bring him up to date on his progress with the case.

When Basel got into the chief's office and sat down, he asked sarcastically, "Now that you have enough time to devote to your other cases, I have an idea. We don't have a clue as to who the perps are and have no finger prints. It seems a little strange that there was a place on one of the shelves that didn't have a single bottle on it. The bottles were cleared out; all of the scotch."

"Big deal," the chief said returning the sarcasm.

"Sir, two men wouldn't kill for some lousy bottles of liquor, would they?"

"Murders have been committed for less."

The chief suggested, "Let's publish a picture taken from the surveillance tape. Maybe someone will recognize the killer and come forward."

Basel groaned, "I think it will give us zilch, but I guess it's our only hope."

The chief didn't like Basel's attitude so he told him to go back and check the place out thoroughly again.

"You're kidding, aren't you?" Basel complained, disgusted with the chief.

"I'm absolutely serious, now get a move on!"

Basel was furious. He kicked at the wall as he left the chief's office and pain shot from his foot to his thigh. "Ouch!" he cried as he hobbled down the hall.

The picture in the newspaper was slightly blurred but it was enough to prompt approximately fifty calls. The chief picked the ten most promising ones, he and Murphy would personally call those.

The first person they called in was an old man with coke bottle glasses; obviously he couldn't see five feet ahead of him. They decided this fellow just wanted some company.

The second was a blonde floozy that answered the door in a satin bathrobe that gaped at the neckline exposing her ample breasts. Murphy's eyes nearly popped out of his head and he couldn't say a word. The chief wanted to burst out laughing but grabbed his arm and they left in a hurry.

The next two tips weren't productive either, but the fifth was different. After introducing themselves to the pudgy man at the door, he invited them into the house.

He told the chief and Murphy that he had witnessed the whole thing go down. "It was about nine at night and I was outside smoking my cigar when a Chevrolet pulled up to the store. Two men got out of the car and went in. Not ten minutes later I heard gunshots. The two guys ran out, jumped in the car and drove away." He paused a minute then added, "I almost forgot, one of them carried out a box of liquor!"

Now the chief knew he was legit. "You didn't happen to get a license plate number did you?" he asked the man hopefully.

"Not all of it, but I saw it was out of state, Ohio I think."

The chief asked, "Can you describe the men?"

"Yup, one was tall, with shoulder length blonde hair. The other one was shorter and was slight of build."

"Clothes?"

"Both wore jeans. The smaller one wore ankle length boots, the bigger one had on deck shoes."

"You have some kind of memory!" Murphy complimented him.

"I was in the military behind the lines. There if you miss a small thing, you can wind up dead."

The chief reached out and shook the man's hand. "Thank you Sir," he said. "You've been a lot of help."

"Would you like a brewski before you leave?"

Murphy was about to answer yes but the chief cut him off by saying, "No, but we may need to speak to you again."

"Any time. You're Grand Junction's finest, aren't you?"

CHAPTER

87

Horace was also scrutinizing the picture in the paper. He looked at it twice, then got out a magnifying glass and looked at it again. Now he was sure. The image of the tall man was Jimmy. The other one looked like Rick. Horace was fuming he was so angry. No wonder his no good son had run away from the authorities; he was a wanted man.

He also thought Jimmy could be the Mafia's hit man that they were looking for. Horace felt sick to his stomach but he knew his son had to be apprehended. No man should be available to kill for money and made up his mind to do something about it.

Horace went into the kitchen and got a roll of paper towels. He dialed the number of the station and then placed the towel over the phone. The dispatcher answered and Horace asked for the chief in a disguised voice, speaking through the paper towel.

The chief answered and Horace quickly said, "I know who the man you're looking for is. I believe he is a Mafia hit man."

"Who is this?" the chief demanded.

Horace hung up as tears came into his eyes. Who would think things would come to this? One thing for sure, he wasn't going to tell his wife or his daughter what Jimmy had done.

About ten minutes later, Horace's phone rang and it was the chief. "I've got a job for you," he said.

Horace knew what was coming and wondered what excuse he could make. "What is it chief?" he asked trying to sound normal.

"Do you still have your Mafia connection?"

"I'm sorry chief, he's no longer there; God bless his soul. He messed up and you know what happens then," he lied.

"Son-of-a-bitch. I got an anonymous phone call identifying one of the hitmen. I thought you could help me identify him."

"Gee chief, I'm sorry but my wife is ill and I'm leaving for Florida as soon as I can." Horace was untruthful but felt he had no choice.

The chief sighed. "I get one step ahead and another one back. I hope your wife gets well soon. When you get back, stop in and see me."

"I will," Horace said feeling guilty for lying. He sat down, wondering where his wayward son could be, until he came up with the idea that he may be at his great Aunt Norma's. As a boy, Jimmy had spent summers with her. She doted on the boy and to her he could do no wrong. She was up in the years now but would welcome him anytime.

CHAPTER

88

Jimmy knocked loudly on the door because he knew his Aunt Norma was hard of hearing. She opened the door and stood there with her auburn hair curling around her face, looking years younger than her age. However, her voice betrayed her as it cracked when she exclaimed, "Jimmy, is that you? It's been ages since I've seen you!" He walked over and hugged her.

"I had some time off from my job and I thought it was time I came to visit you."

"Come in, come in! You can stay as long as you'd like." She paused then asked, "Does your father know where you are?"

"Auntie, I'm a big boy now. I don't have to report to him anymore," Jimmy answered her.

A small gray cat appeared from nowhere and wound itself around her ankles. "Oh dear, here's Snookums, she's my little roommate."

Jimmy stepped back. He hated cats and Norma had one in her house! "How old is it?" he asked.

"Snook-ums," his aunt corrected him.

"I'm allergic to cats," he said sourly.

"Oh dear, I don't know what to do," she said destitute.

"Can't you put her in a kennel while I'm here?" Jimmy asked, irritated.

"Good heavens no, this is Snook-um's house. She even sleeps on my bed."

"In that case, I can't stay here," Jimmy said walking down the steps.

"Oh Jimmy, please don't go," Norma begged.

"I know when I'm not wanted. I'll see you in about twenty years old lady, that's if you live that long," he snarled, wanting to hurt her. If she wasn't who she was he thought, I'd put a knife through her heart and watch her die. He got in his car, backed down the driveway and sped away.

Norma watched him leave and a shiver ran up and down her arms. What kind of monster had he become? She decided to call Horace and tell him about the visit, which she did the next day, telling him the whole sad story.

Horace felt a great relief; at least Jimmy hadn't hurt her. "Where did he go," he asked Norma.

"I don't know, but I'm sure he won't come back here."

"Why?" Horace asked.

"Because he was very nasty before he left. Never mind, at least I'm alive to live another year."

"Don't worry, Norma, you'll live to be a hundred years young," Horace said trying to lighten the mood. "I'll stop by and see you soon, I promise."

"Promises, promises, that's all I get," she answered. "When I see you, I'll believe it," she returned and hung up the phone.

All Horace could think of, was how to alert the chief as to where Jimmy was. He surely couldn't make an anonymous phone call again.

Horace thought back to his days of defending the Mafia and couldn't believe he had come out of it unscathed. On some of the murder one cases, he'd found a way to get them off the hook. He shuddered to think what would have happened to him if he hadn't.

It would not be so, with the hired hitman who had fallen out of their graces. There was a manhunt for him now, for his son Jimmy. He was sure the Mafia was hot on his trail too, because he had absconded with some of their funds. God help him if he gets caught Horace thought.

CHAPTER

89

Rock looked at the pictures of the liquor store robbery suspects that were in the newspaper. At first he thought he was seeing things, but after looking closer, he was positive the smaller man was Rick. He knew Rick was capable of a lot of things, but murder? He looked again at the larger man but didn't recognize him. He knew Rick had been arrested and was confined in jail. Rock decided to visit him there and see if he could find out anything. Of course he wouldn't mention it to Ellen. What she didn't know wouldn't hurt her.

When the chief walked in the station the following day, he found Rock standing at the counter talking to a deputy. He paused to listen to the two men's conversation. "Why do you want to see Rick?" the chief asked Rock point blank.

"I've known him for years and thought I'd see what he has to say."

The chief looked at Rock and said, "I remember you. You took the fall for that Brink's robbery didn't you? We never found out who the other guys were. Care to enlighten me?"

"I did my time, now I just want to get on with my life," Rock returned.

"Alight, Ok," the chief replied, dropping the subject. "I'll let you see him, but I'll go with you."

"I don't think so," Rock said turning around to leave.

"Wait a minute. I'll be like a fly on the wall; I won't say anything." It was all Rock could hope for so he agreed.

"Come on then," the chief said, "The jail is this way."

Rick's cell was 10x10 with a bunk bed and stainless steel toilet and small sink. He was sitting on the bed when the chief unlocked the cage door. He looked up and laughed uproariously. "Look, I've got company!" he said laughing.

"Hello Rick, I heard you were here and thought I'd stop and see you," Rock said.

"Why?" he asked. "We were never friends."

"I disagree. We used to play poker every week, didn't we?"

Rick started to laugh again. "That was before you went to prison."

Rock bristled but tried to stay calm. "Yeah, that was before I took the rap for you guys." The chief looked on with interest; perhaps he would learn something by this this exchange of wits.

"You planned the whole thing!" Rick cried.

"Bull shit!" Rock returned, obviously angry. "You know the coach did. I never wanted any part of it!"

Suddenly, Rick jumped up and raised his fists ready to punch Rock and yelled, "Pow!" and he convulsed with laughter again.

Rock turned to the chief, "Is he always like this?" he asked.

"Yes, he seems to think everything is funny. A psychiatrist will be here tomorrow to evaluate him."

Rick had lost all interest in them as he sat down on the bed and pretended to read while he smiled broadly and mumbled to himself.

"Has he lost his mind?" Rock asked the chief.

"He's nuttier than a fruit cake! But the shrink will tell us more after his visit," the chief replied.

Rock was upset all the way home. He was never a fan of Rick's but he hated to see how the man had regressed. He hoped he'd filled in some of the blanks for the chief. Now he would know who framed him for the burglary. But there was no one for the chief to press charges against, only he and Rick were left. I have done my time and Rick was near insanity. He thought the chief would most likely end the investigation and then close the file on the Brink's robbery case, for good.

CHAPTER

90

Marie came into the office in a great mood every day. She was eager to get to work and became a good employee. Ellen was happy with this change because Marie's work had been getting behind, but it also made her wonder what had caused this new attitude.

Rock told Ellen about Marie's dating the boy next door and that he surmised the relationship was going well. Ellen was curious so she asked Marie if anything was new, like had she met her neighbor?

At first Marie denied her romance with Steven but her face flushed a bright red when she answered Ellen's question.

"Come on Marie, you're Rock's daughter. Don't you think he would know what's going on?"

"I'm a big girl," Marie hedged.

"Have it your way then," Ellen laughed. "Now let's get to work." Ellen's good mood lasted until she got home that evening and told Rock the story. He didn't seem surprised when she told him how Marie was acting. Rather, he said he knew of the affair and wasn't happy about it.

"Why?" Ellen countered. What was Rock talking about?

"Are you aware that Steven has moved in with her?"

Ellen was surprised. "When did this happen?"

"A month ago, give or take. I don't like it. Steven has a reputation of being wild."

"Romance has a way of settling people down."

"A leopard doesn't change its spots," Rock insisted. "Rumor has it he's seeing the Hall girl on the side."

"I hope he has the sense to use protection. All Marie needs is to get pregnant again," Ellen added. "You will have to talk to her, the sooner the better."

Rock agreed. "Tonight's the night. I'll let you know what I find out."

Marie opened the door when Rock knocked on it. He could tell she had been crying. "What's the problem honey?" he asked her.

"Steven walked out and isn't coming back," she sobbed. "Come in Dad, I need to talk to someone." Marie's tears subsided as she began talking. "According to him, I don't do anything right. I don't cook what he likes, I don't clean the house enough and I don't fold his clothes right. I tried talking to his parents but they wouldn't listen. His father indicated this wasn't the first time he's done something like this and his mother called him a spoiled brat."

"If I get ahold of the jerk, I'll punch him out. He won't be able to chase around for a long time," Rock threatened.

"No don't do it Dad," Marie said then realized what he had said. "What did you mean by chase around?"

"With Gracie Hall, rumor has it she is pregnant with his child."

Marie began to sob again. "I don't believe it!" she exclaimed. "He sleeps with me every night."

"You're being foolish. The Hall girl is a loose girl and has had a kid before."

Marie wailed and said again, "I will not believe it!"

"Pack up your things; you're coming home with me. I won't let you stay in this house another minute."

"But it's my house," Marie cried.

"We'll put it up for rent. Strangers can stay here until Steven moves. My guess is he won't stay long." Marie cried the whole time she got her clothes together. "I'll get in touch with the chief to see if his deputies would watch over the house. Steven doesn't have a key does he?" Marie nodded yes. "You're a fool! We'll make sure the locks are changed too."

Rock led Marie out of the house, wondering how he could calm her down.

Rusty did it for him. When he saw Marie he wiggled all over and tried to jump up on her. As usual Marie petted him when he put his head in her lap. She stopped crying and actually looked happy.

Rock told Rusty, "I want you to be a good boy. You'll have to share with your sister for a while." Rock was sure the dog nodded his head in agreement.

CHAPTER

91

The psychiatrist tried to talk to Rick but all he did was laugh and wouldn't answer his questions. He told the chief that he was sure the judge would declare Rick incompetent to stand trial and would recommend his being confined to a state mental institution until he was well and could be tried for his crimes.

The chief wasn't surprised and immediately made arrangements to transfer him. Rick became violent when he heard the news and was put into a straight-jacket so they were able to move him.

Once at Glenview, Rick continued his erratic behavior, laughing or screaming all the time. A doctor asked if he'd had a stroke. "No, he's just been laughing and hasn't stopped. He wouldn't answer any questions for the psychiatrist's interview either. He diagnosed him as a manic-depressive schizophrenic. All we can do is put him in solitary confinement until he calms down. There he will be evaluated daily until we see what ward we should place him in."

"Will you let me know how he progresses?" the chief asked. "We are waiting to see if he will be competent to stand trial."

"Some people improve, others never do. We'll just have to see. I'll keep you updated on what the situation is chief."

CHAPTER

92

Jimmy wasn't about to use his cell phone because of the GPS showing his location, so he stopped at 7-Eleven to use the pay phone. He had the number of a retired hitman who told him that if he ever got into a jam he should call him.

The phone was answered on the second ring. "You got Jake. Who's calling?"

"Hey man, it's Jimmy."

"Hey, how yah been?"

"Fine, but I need a favor."

"Oh, what did you do?"

"I owe the boss five grand that I need to pay back so I'm on the run."

"You can't pay him now?"

"I told them I would do another job to work it off, but I couldn't get it done."

"Oh Man, you're dead if they find you."

"That's where you come in. I'd like you to find me a place to crash until the heat is off."

"Give me a day to think about it. I'll get back to you."

"I don't think I can do that. They're hot on my trail and they know the approximate area I'm in."

"Jesus, Jimmy! I'll let you stay at my place tonight, but that's it. I don't want any problem with the Mafia."

"You'll have to direct me to your place. I know it is a secret, but you know I won't say anything."

"Alright, here it is," and Jake explained how to find him. Jimmy took off in a hurry, anxious to get there.

That night Jake and Jimmy drove to an old police safe house, nestled in a copse of trees, about ten miles from town. It was stocked with enough food for a month, most likely all the time Jimmy would need. He intended to go to Canada after that, he didn't think the Mafia would look for him there.

CHAPTER

93

Tracy called Glenview several times a day to see how Rick was. The head nurses got so tired of taking her calls they didn't answer them anymore. Frustrated, Tracy begged her father to take her over to see him. At first he refused, but later relented.

Horace went up to the counter and asked what room Rick was in. The woman behind the desk didn't reply but pressed a button and soon a nurse appeared. "We came to see Rick Rayburn," Horace said.

"I'm sorry Sir, but Mr. Rayburn can't have visitors," she replied firmly.

Tracy spoke up, "I'm his wife," she said.

The nurse turned, "It's against the rules. But if you insist!" She led them down a long hallway past several rooms with patients in, then stopped before a closed door and turned to them, "Don't expect too much," she warned.

When the three of them entered the room, Rick was staring out the window and didn't move. "You have visitors," the nurse said." Tracy and Horace waited patiently until he turned around. Rick was still dressed in his pajamas and slippers.

Tracy ran to him with her arms out ready to hug him. Rick looked up and muttered, "Who are you?"

Tracy was aghast. "I'm your wife Rick," she cried. She looked at Horace and put a hand on Rick's shoulder.

"Why don't you go outside, I'll try to talk to him," Horace suggested. "Hey Rick, remember me? I'm Tracy's father," he asked him. Rick's eyes fluttered but he didn't speak.

It's no use, just as I thought," the nurse said quietly. "That will be enough for today; we don't want him to get agitated."

Horace looked at Rick and saw his hands shaking and his head looked like it was on a swivel. He asked the nurse, "Can we bring his kids here net time? They are very close to him."

"No, he wouldn't know them either and you wouldn't want them to see their father like this, would you?" Horace shook his head no.

On the way home neither one of them spoke, as both were lost in their own thoughts. Neither one of them ever wanted to go back there again.

CHAPTER

94

Marie settled into the house with Rock and Ellen. Everything went fine until Steven began to harass her. He called her night and day until Rock had him blocked so he couldn't get through any longer. He tried looking into Marie's bedroom window at night until Rusty caught him and bit him in the leg. After that he left Marie alone except for sending her several texts a day. Then he started stalking Marie when she was on her way to work and sat across the street watching the real estate office. After that Marie rode to work with Ellen. Then he proceeded to ring the doorbell day and night. Rock complained that Steven never slept. Marie was afraid to leave the house without someone with her.

Finally, Rock decided to report him to the chief who said he would take care of it. That stopped Steven from harassing Marie and the household returned to normal.

Rock always read the morning newspaper before he went to work. An article caught his eye and he couldn't wait to show it to Marie. There was an engagement picture of Steven and Gracie Hall holding hands. It appeared that Steven was gone for good and wouldn't bother Marie again.

CHAPTER

95

Horace usually talked to his wife every day. When he hadn't heard from her for several days he became worried and his imagination ran wild. Was she ill? Why wasn't she calling him? He started calling their home several times a day, but there was never an answer.

He called Delta airlines and made a reservation to fly to Tampa the following week. Horace hated to leave his daughter when she was distraught, but he had been married to his wife for sixty years and she had to be his first priority. When his granddaughter Susie begged him to stay, it almost broke his heart but he knew he had to go.

In desperation, Horace placed one last call to his home. The phone rang and rang, still there was no answer.

Finally, a woman's shaky voice answered, "Hello Horace," his wife said. There wasn't any affection in her voice; it was like she was talking to a stranger.

Horace was instantly on alert. "What's wrong Sybil, are you sick?"

"No, no it's not that."

"What is it then?" Horace asked puzzled.

"It's nothing," she answered vaguely.

Horace became upset. "What's wrong with you?" he hollered. He could tell that she had her hand over the phone, but her voice sounded muffled. "God damn-it, what is wrong?" he demanded.

"He's here," she whispered.

"Who is there?"

Instead of answering his question, she said brightly, "Tell me, how is little Billy?"

Horace got the picture. It was someone Sybil was afraid of that was in the house with her. "Listen carefully," he told her. "Don't act scared, be friendly and don't antagonize him in any way." As an after-thought, he asked her, "Do you know him?"

She murmured a quiet, "Yes."

Horace had a bad feeling and wondered who could be there, other than a member of the Mafia. "Is he the Mafia?" he demanded.

"You know him," she replied, then quickly said, "I've got to go now," and hung up.

Suddenly Horace realized who it had to be. There was no one in the Mafia that knew him personally except one person. It was the man who'd been his contact for years. "I thought Joe was dead!" he exclaimed out loud. But if he was at his house he must be running from them and it wouldn't be long before they figured out where he was.

Horace ran into the bedroom, opened his suitcase and threw his clothes into it, not caring what condition they were in. Twenty minutes later he was out the door and on his way to the airport. There were several flights to Tampa and he'd catch one. He'd pay any price he had to.

CHAPTER

96

Tracy was beside herself. She felt sorry for Rick because he was confined in such an awful place, surrounded with only nutcases. On top of that the kids were nagging her to go and see their father. Finally she decided to take them up to see him regardless of what the rules were.

So after school she told them she was taking them out for an ice cream cone. Because ice cream was their most favorite thing in the world, they were overjoyed to be getting the treat. Instead Tracy drove right past the A&W and their faces fell.

"Where are you going?" little Billy demanded.

"It's a surprise," Tracy told them. When she turned into Glenview they perked up.

"Are we going to see Dad?" Patty asked excitedly.

"We sure are," Tracy answered, hoping everything would go alright.

The same nurse greeted them as before, but with a frown on her face. "I told you not to bring the kids, didn't I?" She sighed deeply, "Alright, I'll take you in, but expect the worst."

Tracy and the kids followed her down the same path she and her father had taken before. When they walked in, Rick jumped up from the chair where he sat and stared at the kids. "Come here," he said looking overjoyed to see them. Tracy watched with delight. Rick even called them by name, but didn't seem to recognize her yet.

By the expression on the nurse's face, she could tell that she didn't believe what was happening. She'd been told by the doctor that Rick was making remarkable progress but hadn't realized how far he'd come.

The kids chattered about school and told him they missed him. When they prepared to leave, Billy asked him when he was coming home. Rick shook his head and his eyes misted. "I don't know," he said mournfully.

It was hard to say good-bye. On the way home, Tracy bought ice cream cones for them and like children do, they forgot about the disappointment of visiting their father. The whole thing bummed out Tracy because Rick looked like he was so well. That night she cooked the kids their favorite meal, hot dogs on the grill. She now realized how much she'd neglected Billy and Patty, and made up her mind to be a better mom.

After that, she took the kids to see Rick often and was happy that he seemed better each time. She was sure he would be released soon, but knew he would then be declared competent to stand trial and would be sentenced to prison for a long time.

When Horace got to Tampa he hailed a cab and was at his house in minutes. Sybil greeted him at the door and didn't look like herself at all. "Where is Joe?" he asked her.

"Oh, he's staying at a local motel until you returned. I found out he wasn't dangerous and it actually was pleasant having him for company while you were gone."

Horace was surprised at her change of attitude. "When can I see him?" he asked.

"Joe said you should call him immediately when you got home." In spite of himself, Horace said he would be glad to see him. After all, they'd gone through Hell together while they were associated with the mob.

CHAPTER

97

It wasn't long before Steven got into trouble. He was caught robbing a gas station and thrown in jail leaving his new wife and infant to fend for themselves.

His father immediately took them in and also paid a thousand dollar bond for their son. However, they refused to let Steven move in with them and helped his wife file for an annulment.

Because Gracie didn't have an education she couldn't get a high paying job, but finally landed one in a grocery store cashiering at minimum wage. She gave Steven's parents all she earned for room and board. Steven's mother babysat while she worked so she didn't have to pay any money out. They cared more for the baby every day and became very attached to him.

Three months after Gracie moved in, she and her husband broached the idea to Gracie that they would like to adopt the baby. Although the baby's mother resisted the idea, she knew the baby would be better off with them. They would see that he would get an education and have all the good things in life. Besides that, she would have visitation rights and could see her son whenever she wanted to. The adoption wasn't for a month and at that time the Smith's would take over as his legal parents.

It would be five years before Steven would get out of prison. Even given an early release, he wouldn't get out for at least three years. By that time they were sure Steven would get visitation rights.

When the baby was a year old it was obvious there was something wrong with little Chad. One night the baby cried and cried and wouldn't stop. Mrs. Smith jumped up from her bed and found he was struggling to breath. She took him out of his crib and tried to soothe him but grew concerned when the boy began turning blue. She screamed for her husband and together they rushed the baby to the hospital.

The doctor examined him and told the worried couple that he had a severe case of asthma and that he would be plagued with it all his life. He explained what they would have to do for the prevention of a severe attack but said it could be controlled.

They felt better after the doctor cleaned out the baby's lungs and gave him medication. Almost instantly Chad began breathing normally and his skin returned to its natural color. Relieved, the Smith's took the baby home. His adoptive mother thanked God he was all right.

CHAPTER

98

B asel went back to the liquor store to try to find new evidence; he felt sure he had missed something.

Sure enough, he found a man's glove partially under the shelf that held the liquor. He tried it on, but it was too small. Then he quickly placed it in a bag, but as he did it, he knew he shouldn't have touched it. The chief would throw a fit when he found out his finger prints were on it. But he might as well come clean, tell the chief and take the shit. At least he'd found some evidence they didn't have before.

Instead of getting angry when Basel told him of his mistake, the chief praised him. He knew exactly whose glove this was. The canine had found the matching glove when he was used to apprehend Rick. This was evidence that Rick had been at the liquor store murder. This was another charge to add to his long list of crimes. The chief hoped Rick would be deemed out of his mind and be ordered to stay in the hospital forever.

As for Tracy, Horace had talked her into flying with her children to Florida to stay with him and Sybil for a while. It was his intent to have the children be enrolled in a school in Tampa, and he would urge Tracy to find work. With their roots firmly planted, Horace thought after time, she would want to stay.

As it turned out, the family only stayed a few weeks because Rick had escaped from Glenview.

The chief blew his stack when he found out Rick had gotten away. He drove over the speed limit to the hospital at once. When he got there he demanded to see the person in charge.

Soon an elderly nurse appeared and walked over to him. She was obviously at least seventy-five, far past the retirement age. "Hello, Chief," she said in a friendly voice.

The chief had no part of it. He wasn't there on a social call, but on serious business. "Show me to your office," he said curtly. "We have a lot to discuss."

Silently, the nurse did as she was told. When they were seated, the chief wasted no time. "How the hell could Rick get away from here?" he demanded.

"Well," she answered, "We take the patients who are almost ready to go home out for a breath of fresh air on nice days. On this particular day the nurses were all busy, so they let a volunteer take Rick outside in a wheel chair. She was to park him in the sunshine under a tree. It was a warm day and a brisk wind blew. The girl realized she had forgotten to bring him a jacket and didn't want to get in trouble, so she ran back to Rick's room to get one. She wasn't gone for five minutes, but when she got back the wheel chair was empty and he was long gone. Needless to say, the girl got fired, but the damage was done."

The chief got up to leave. "I recommend you get better security around here," he snapped as he left. The nurse looked like she was about to burst into tears. She was afraid her job would be eliminated and she badly needed the money to support herself and her ailing daughter.

An all points alert was put into the computer. The authorities in the area were told to make this missing person a high priority. That was all the chief could do and he felt exasperated. Could he catch a break on this one? He'd never been so despondent in his life. The chief seriously thought of quitting but he only had one year before he could retire, one more, long year.

CHAPTER

99

Rick ran until he was winded, then he trotted. Finally he bent over gasping and he knew he had to rest. He no more than got seated on a large rock when he heard the barking of dogs behind him.

Instantly Rick knew that the police were chasing him. He jumped down and ran for the creek about a half mile away. It hurt him to run but he made it to the water and almost fell in when he landed on the rocky shore. He crossed to the other side of the creek and had just hidden in some woods when he heard the dogs barking at the creek's edge. They were confused because they lost his scent. Rick took off again because he knew the law would negotiate the creek in a minute. He followed a beaten down path until he came to a small gravel road.

Damn he thought, doubting if there would be any traffic on this road. After walking a mile, he was about to rest when a large logging truck rounded the curve ahead of him. Rick stuck out his hand, and to his amazement the truck pulled over. The driver's front door opened and he hollered, "What are you doing on this road? No one uses it anymore!" Not waiting for an answer, he yelled, "Come on, hop in, the nearest town is thirty miles down the road, I'll drop you off. I have to drop my logs at a saw mill there." Rick didn't care where he went and thirty miles was a good spell from Glenview. He could lose himself there.

He was surprised when the trucker let him out by a forest in the middle of nowhere. He explained, "The saw mill is on a small road up yonder a piece."

Those were the first words he'd spoken since Rick joined him in the truck. He wondered if the reason was because he was in his light blue pajamas from Glenview. So what? He thought he'd never see the man again, and was sure because he was just driving through, that he wouldn't squeal on him.

Where should I go now? Rick had lost the taste for hitching, so he walked along the gravel road until he came to a small farm. It was set so far away from the road that he could barely see it. He couldn't believe his eyes when he saw a truck just like the one Jimmy drove sitting in front of the house. There couldn't be two trucks just like that one he thought, with the same rusted sides, faded red in color.

Even if he was afraid of the man, he decided to see if he could take refuge with him. After all, the arrangements would be as good as any alternate he could think of.

Jimmy appeared happy to see him when he opened the door. Rick wasn't buying it because the two hadn't been on good terms when they last saw each other.

When they were seated and each of them had a beer in their hands, Jimmy opened the conversation. "What are you running from?" he asked.

Rick told him the whole sorbid story then waited for Jimmy to reply. "What are you doing right here in the middle of nowhere?" Rick returned.

Jimmy laughed heartily, "Hiding out like you, but I have connections who help me."

"Who? The Mafia?" Rick asked sarcastically.

"Retired," Jimmy replied confidently.

"I wouldn't trust them as far as I could throw them!"

"You have your opinion, I have mine. What say we have another beer?"

The two men drank until they could hardly walk but stumbled to bed then slept until noon. Each night after that, Jimmy and Rick drank and talked themselves stupid until Rick finally got sick of it.

One night, instead of drinking, Rick went outside to sit on an old swing and gaze at the stars. He grew melancholy wishing he could turn back the time and do things differently.

Suddenly Rick heard loud noises in front of the house. Curious he walked around the side of the house and hid in some bushes. At first the discussion between the two guys and Jimmy was congenial but soon it turned ugly. One man shoved Jimmy and the other took out a pistol from his jacket pocket and shot Jimmy point blank in his chest. He fell to the ground without a sound and was silent.

Rick shook with the harshness of it all, but then remembered how many lives Jimmy had taken. He shrunk further back into the bushes, held his breath and prayed the hoodlums wouldn't see him. They walked within three feet from where he crouched, so he could hear what they said. "The goofy bastard," one said. "He brought the story that old Jake had retired from the Mafia. Didn't the fool know that no one leaves them and gets to live long? Poof you're gone in a heartbeat!"

Rick hiked into town in a hurry. He wanted to get as far away as fast as he could. He wanted to tell his father-in-law the story, but Horace didn't like him and wouldn't listen to what he said.

The next thing Rick did was unexplainable. He walked to the first pay phone he saw and called the chief and turned himself in. At first the chief thought it was a hoax but then realized it was really Rick. "Come and get me," he begged. "I want to come back and face the music."

The chief sighed with relief. He felt a confession coming and the liquor store murder case would be closed at last.

The chief bragged to anyone who cared, that he and his deputies had solved both the liquor store murders and the Brink's truck robbery.

Rock was completely exonerated and left alone to enjoy life with Ellen and his family. His paybacks were finished, his revenge was complete.

Ellen's Real estate business flourished. She did so well that she and Rock took a vacation to Europe every year and she was thinking of buying a summer home on the French Riviera.

Marie married a man five years younger than she and gave birth to two boys and a girl.

Sybil and Horace lived a long life well into their eighties and gave a sizeable inheritance to Tracy and her children.

All of them had highs and lows throughout their lives. But at the end of the day, all of them were happy and satisfied with their lives.